# WILD

## Tiger Trouble

**LUCY COURTENAY**

*Coming soon . . .*

WILD
2. Monkey Magic
3. Bear Hug

*More from Hodder Children's Books*

THE PONY WHISPERER
The Word on the Yard
Team Challenge
Runaway Rescue
Prize Problems
Pony Rebellion
Stables SOS
*Janet Rising*

Saffy's Angel
Indigo's Star
Permanent Rose
Caddy Ever After
Forever Rose
Caddy's World
*Hilary McKay*

# Foreword

## by Chris Brown,
## Director of Tooth 'n' Claw

*The UK's premier animal training facility
for film, TV and advertising.*

Just like Tori and Taya in this book, I lived my entire
childhood surrounded by wild animals. Our record at
one point was three chimpanzees, two lions, a bear and
a lazy python. It had always seemed the most natural
thing in the world for my sister and me to wake up
with a lion sleeping at the foot of the bed. Apparently
this is not normal for most children.

Why on earth would anyone want to foster wild
animals, you may ask? The truth is that animals from
Safari parks produce a lot of young that survive in
captivity but would not survive in the wild. Therefore
someone has to look after them, as their natural
mothers are not equipped for a full litter to survive.
We were one of the chosen families tasked with
the challenge.

I am just glad that now I can open my eyes in safety
in the mornings without a jungle beast leaping on
my head!

www.toothnclaw.com

Copyright © 2011 Lucy Courtenay

First published in Great Britain in 2011
by Hodder Children's Books

The right of Lucy Courtenay to be identified as the Author of
the Work has been asserted by her in accordance with the
Copyright, Designs and Patents Act 1988

1

All rights reserved. Apart from any use permitted under UK copyright
law, this publication may only be reproduced, stored or transmitted in
any form, or by any means with prior permission in writing from the
publishers or in the case of reprographic production in accordance with
the terms of licences issued by the Copyright Licensing Agency and may
not be otherwise circulated in any form of binding or cover other than
that in which it is published and without a similar condition being
imposed on the subsequent purchaser.

All characters in this publication are fictitious and any resemblance
to real persons, living or dead, is purely coincidental.

A Catalogue record for this book is available from the British Library

ISBN-13: 978 0 340 99880 9

Typeset in AGaramond by Avon DataSet Ltd,
Bidford on Avon, Warwickshire

Printed and bound in Great Britain by
CPI Bookmarque Ltd, Croydon, Surrey

The paper and board used in this paperback by Hodder Children's Books
are natural recyclable products made from wood grown in
sustainable forests. The manufacturing processes conform to the
environmental regulations of the country of origin.

Hodder Children's Books
a division of Hachette Children's Books
338 Euston Road, London NW1 3BH
An Hachette UK company
www.hachette.co.uk

# 1

## Furry Dustbin Lorry

When a tiger lands on you first thing in the morning, even when they're just four months old, you know about it. Chips's paws are already the same size as my head and he weighs nearly as much as Rabbit, our golden retriever.

'Oooh!'

Chips was straddling my head. I could see his furry white tummy up close. Part of me wanted to cuddle him because he is SO gorgeous. The rest of me wanted to breathe. Breathing won.

'No licking,' I gasped, laughing and kissing Chips's rough black nose while trying to avoid his tongue. Tiger tongues are like sandpaper and can lick polish off toenails.

'Keep it down, Taya, will you?' yawned Tori from the other side of our bedroom.

Don't start me on how uncool sharing a bedroom with your hideous twin sister is. Let's just say that if it was down to me, Tori would be in the garden shed.

'It's not me,' I protested, still wrestling with the cubling. 'It's Chips! I didn't hear him come in. Was he sleeping on your bed again? You know how Mum feels about that. I hope for your sake—'

Tori suddenly screamed.

Chips reversed off me like a furry dustbin lorry and hurtled for the bedroom door, his orange and black tail whizzing after him. It made me think of those stripy rocket balloons that go mad when you let them go.

'My duvet!' my twin sister yelled furiously down the stairs. 'MUM! Chips has just . . .'

I'll leave you to imagine what Chips had just done to Tori's duvet.

Mum fosters wild animals at home for zoos and safari parks. Crazy but cool, right? When she left her first career (she was a MODEL! Seriously!) she got a zoology degree and a Dangerous Wild Animals licence and brought a pair of orphaned tiger cubs home from Wild World, our local safari park. She called them Salt and

Vinegar and had them until they grew too big and started eating the carpet. When they went back, the park keepers said they'd never seen such healthy young animals and what had Mum been feeding them on and could they borrow the recipe? And that's how it all began, and why Tori and I have always had wild animals in our house.

Wild animals – yes. Tigers – no. Tori and I weren't born in the days of Salt and Vinegar. So imagine our excitement when the Chips and Gravy saga kicked off.

It was just Mum and us in the house when the phone call came. Dad was away on one of his animal photography jobs, somewhere in China. Tori and I were finishing our homework and I was trying to draw snails on her book when she wasn't looking. Tori's easy to wind up. She winds me up too, more than I would like. That's the trouble with being twins from entirely different planets.

The first sign that the phone call was an AIN – Animal In Need – was when Mum put the phone down and burst into tears.

Mum is very emotional, like me. She's been getting AIN calls for thirteen years, but she never gets used to them. She goes through four stages.

Stage One: Tears.

Stage Two: Silence.

Stage Three: Rage and Insults on Behalf of the Animal.

Stage Four is the bit I like to call 'Let's do the show right here!', after these old black and white films we have on DVD. It's the stage where Mum mops her eyes and pushes up her sleeves and starts ordering extra weaning bottles and food and equipment and booking specialist vets.

Tori and I waited for Stages One and Two to pass. As Mum started to wind herself into Stage Three, we moved in and put our arms round her. We've had lots of practice at timing this just right. My sister and I don't agree about much, but where Mum and our animals are concerned, we don't argue.

'This idiot has a new wife who wants a pet tiger,' Mum hissed. 'This *criminal* idiot pays money to a stranger he meets in India. This *flea-brained criminal* idiot smuggles two newborn cubs to his house in Jersey on his oh-so-private plane and gives them to his wife. In a box. With *ribbons*.'

Tori looked as sick as I felt. Baby animals, stolen from their mother and tied up in a box like a diamond ring? What sort of person would do that? Just the thought of it made me want to cry too.

'Of course, this wife doesn't know what to do with them. She tries to feed them on cow's milk. The babies are starving. Their bones are showing through their fur. They are dehydrated. Their eyes are infected. They have not got long to live.'

Now I was feeling *really* sick.

'This thief calls the vet. The vet calls the police and the thief is taken away for questioning.'

'In chains, I hope,' Tori said in an ultra-cold voice.

I was thinking more along the lines of a box with ribbons that can't be untied.

'After the police take away this thief, the vet calls Wild World. And Wild World calls me.' Mum looked at us both with tears shimmering in her big brown eyes. 'They are coming to us tomorrow morning.'

Oh my wombats! Tigers are completely and utterly the best animals ever in the entire whole world and their cubs are that times a million. Mum had fostered a few cubs over the years: a cheetah with the cutest little bogbrush face, a serval, an Iberian lynx that chewed up my shoes because it liked the taste of the leather. And now Tori and I were about to get our first tigers EVER!

'How long will we have them?' I asked breathlessly.

'Six months, maybe more,' said Mum.

'Outside?' Tori checked. 'In our garden cages?'

Mum shook her head. 'They are too young for that. We'll have to have them with us in the house until they're four or five months.'

'Suits me,' said Tori.

'Me too,' I said, when I'd finished hyperventilating. Tigers! In my house! It was almost too much to think about. Just wait till Dad came home from China! What would he say?

Mum was already moving into Stage Four. She is such a professional. 'With your father away, I need your help,' she warned us. 'It means not much sleep, because we will feed them through the night. It means no going out with your friends until Dad comes home because we can't leave the babies alone for a second. They are too young and fragile. Will you do this for me?'

'YES, Mum!' I cried. 'Like, seriously, yes! Totally and completely yes. Yessville. Yesseroo. Yes, yes, yes!'

'Sure,' said Tori.

You can see why I find my sister annoying.

That night I was too excited to go to sleep.

'We should call them something like Salt and Vinegar, in keeping with family tradition,' I said. 'Two names that go together completely perfectly. Sparkle and Lipgloss?'

On the other side of the room, Tori made a retching noise. 'Sparkle and Lipgloss? Please!'

'Fine,' I said, annoyed already. 'You think of something better.'

'Nebula and Supernova.'

I snorted. 'Trust you to get all scientific.'

'Spell it,' said Tori.

'What?'

'Scientific. Since you so clearly know what you're talking about, let's hear you spell it.'

'You're changing the subject,' I said hotly. Tori knew I had as much chance of spelling scientific as growing a pair of tiger whiskers. 'We don't know what sex they are yet, so we probably need something a bit more general. Um . . . Apple and Crumble? Jelly and Custard?'

'Chips and Gravy.'

I propped myself up on my elbow. Much as I hated to admit it, Tori was on to something. 'Chips and Gravy,' I said reluctantly. 'It's quite good, I suppose.'

'I'm blushing at your effusiveness,' said Tori.

I had no idea what effusiveness was, but there was no way I was going to ask. So I changed the subject.

'Do they have stripes when they're babies?'

'Spots,' said Tori.

I stared through the darkness at my sister's bed. 'How come?' I said in amazement.

'Of course they have stripes, you doughnut,' Tori said.

I hated it when Tor reeled me in like that.

'I just thought maybe they were like Dalmatians,' I said defensively. 'Getting their patterns a bit later. You don't have to be all funny about it.'

Tor was quiet for a bit.

'Do you ever think about school in September?' she said out of nowhere.

I was still brooding over the spotty tiger cub thing. 'No,' I muttered. 'Because I'm not a swot like you.'

It was May and we were in our last term at our primary school, Castle Hill, busy being the biggest kids in the playground and planning the upcoming obstacle race at sports day and thinking about how Zoe McGuigan had just got a new hamster. Secondary school was still as far away as Christmas.

'Did you know there's going to be three hundred kids in our year?' Tori said.

'Yeah, right.' I wasn't falling for another of Tor's wind-ups.

'And only us and that Joe Morton in Mr Thompson's class from Castle Hill,' Tori went on.

I couldn't even picture Joe Morton. Was he the skinny one with massive ears or the kid with an earring that went putrid in Year Four? Still unsure about whether Tori was joking, I decided to get things back on safer ground.

'How big do you think the cubs are going to be?' I tried to picture the little mewling balls. 'Will we be able to fit one in each hand?'

'What are you going to do, juggle with them?'

I flung myself back on my pillow as, once again, Tori's voice went all scornful. Why were we twins? Why were we identical to look at when we were so different underneath? Why were we even related?

The cubs arrived before the postman the next day. Our dog, Rabbit, went mental. She's mad about the animals Mum brings back and always goes into Mother Mode. That's golden retrievers for you.

I pushed Rabbit's eager nose out of the way as I stared in awe at Chips, cradling him very carefully. His eyes were still quite crusty and he felt thin, but he was magical. He yawned, showing little gums and a long pink tongue. Despite myself, I double-checked the pattern on his fur. Yup. Stripes.

'Tori, you hold Gravy.' Mum handed the other cub to my sister. 'I must get their first feed ready.'

Tori and I sat side by side, holding our precious bundles. Amazingly, I felt no urge to talk. A moment of rare twinly union fell on us as we stared at the two fluffy miracles in our hands.

Mum bustled about, mixing the right proportions of powdered milk and a few drops of extra glucose before testing the temperature of the cubs' feed on her upturned wrist. You know how I said Mum was really emotional? When she is looking after our animals, her emotional side gives way to this complete calmness that makes me think of a deep, still, warm lagoon.

'Can we feed them?' begged Tori. 'It's only seven, and Zoe's mum won't collect us for another hour and a half. Can we? Please?'

Because Mum needed to be with the cubs, we were being taken to school by Zoe McGuigan's mum for the rest of the week, until Dad came back from China at the weekend and could take over.

'They are still quite dehydrated, so don't squeeze in too much milk at a time,' said Mum, handing us a dropper each.

Chips squirmed in my hand and made the most

adorable little squeaking noise. I held the little dropper very carefully and tucked the end into his mouth, squeezing the rubber bulb on the end as gently as I could. He spluttered, losing half of it down his fluffy white front. But it wasn't long before he got the idea.

When the cubs had finished feeding, Gravy fell asleep. Mum took them both and quickly checked what was left of their umbilical cords, wiping them with disinfectant.

'See what Rabbit thinks of them,' she said.

We offered Rabbit the cubs, who had both now fallen asleep with their little feet sticking straight up in the air. Rabbit got all excited and licked them both. The cubs both wriggled happily. It felt like they were home.

# A Massive Brick Rat

So. Back to our bedroom four months on with its whiff of tiger wee. Dad was back from a recent trip to Malaysia, and Chips and Gravy were both bigger than your average dog. It was an inset Monday, so Tori and I were planning to play with them all day long. Cubs love play. Just like humans, it's how tiger babies learn about life.

Tori pulled the soggy *Doctor Who* duvet off her bed with a shout of disgust. The smell floated across the room, even though it's a big room and I'm at one end under the window and Tori's at the other end by the fireplace. I wrinkled my nose.

'Gravy would never do that on my bed,' complained Tori.

'You never let Gravy *on* your bed,' I pointed out, 'because last time you did he ripped a hole in the Tardis. "Where Cybermen failed, one tiger cub succeeded",' I added in what I thought was quite a good Doctor Who impression.

Tori gave me her most withering look. My twin believes the Doctor is God. She's the sort of person who knows all about the solar system, and how time travel really is possible if you do it a certain way, and why our microwave destroys my frankfurters but always does hers perfectly.

'Bet you wish Chips had done it on my bed instead,' I said, smoothing my pink, sparkly duvet with one hand.

'Your duvet's wet enough without Chips adding to its problems,' said Tori.

Mum steamed into our room. 'How many times have I told you not to let the tigers on either of your beds?' she demanded. 'Both of you, out of bed and downstairs. The tigers need a walk and we don't have any defrosted mice for breakfast.'

Before you get any weird ideas – OK, any ideas weirder than the ones you're probably already having – *we* don't eat mice for breakfast. Our ball python, Fernando, does.

Our house needs quite a lot of explaining. It's like someone once put a pile of bricks down in a heap and stuck them together at weird angles while maybe listening in a distracted kind of way to a football match on the radio or whatever builders listened to a hundred years ago. It's a total mess, inside and out. Mum bought it with her modelling money a million years ago, well before she met Dad and we came along. She bought it because it backs on to Fernleigh Common, which backs on to Wild World. Of course, it's perfectly safe for our animals – Mum has to renew her Dangerous Wild Animals licence every year and gets checked on all the time. But when you've got animals wandering around, there's not much point in having posh sofa covers and nice carpets.

Things had got worse since Chips and Gravy moved in. Just as Mum had warned us, they had lived in our house like massive pussycats, sleeping anywhere they fancied and scratching up the banister posts. Right now, not only was our house your basic catastrophe, it looked like someone was burgling it regularly.

The kitchen is especially bad. The cupboards are brown wood and the tiles have orange flowers on. The range cooker is older than Mum, and croaks like a frog sometimes when the oil supply gets air bubbles in it. There are boxes of animal food and bottles and bowls all dangling off shelves over the sink. The table in the middle of the room is stained with mug marks, the chairs don't match and the floor is covered in black and white lino that curls up at the edges, sometimes with a nice frilly line where the tigers have chewed it. It's basically a disaster area.

There's a big photo on the least horrible wall in our kitchen, of Mum in her modelling days. She's wearing Ray-Bans and her hair is as big as a Newfoundland dog. I don't mind saying it: our mother is probably the most beautiful woman in the whole world. She's called Anita and she's Portuguese and she's got long hair that pours over her shoulders like melted chocolate, big brown eyes and skin the colour of Victoria Beckham's, only real. I wish we looked like her. Tori doesn't care about stuff like that, being Tori. But, apart from having dark-brown hair and eyes, Tori and I take after Dad. Tall, pale and very English. Only without beards, obviously.

I looked from the picture to the real thing sitting with her coffee and cereal and newspaper, and decided to try the Conversation again.

'This place needs a makeover,' I began, like I did

each time I started the Conversation.

'It's perfect,' said Mum, just like she always did each time I started the Conversation. She turned over a page in her paper.

'You can get really cheap kitchens with washing machines and microwaves and everything included at the moment,' I said hopefully.

'You can't warm baby animals in a microwave,' Mum pointed out.

'You can if they're frozen mice,' I said. I had just defrosted Fernando's breakfast, so I knew what I was talking about.

'Your father's photographs pay for our food and our house,' Mum said patiently. 'The money I get from Wild World pays for the animals' feed, care, licences, insurance and vet bills. We don't have anything left for a new kitchen, Taya.'

Chips gave a loud yawn and turned over in Rabbit's basket. Now he and Gravy were both lying upside down with their tummies in the air. There was hardly room for one of them in the basket these days, let alone both. Rabbit didn't stand a chance of squeezing in too, and was lying under the kitchen table instead. You could tell she was there because you could hear her tail thumping against the floor.

'I have warmed a hundred baby animals in the bottom oven of the range, kissed your father a thousand times at that sink and changed your and Tori's nappies a million times on this table,' Mum went on. 'Why do I want it to be different?'

Deep down, I didn't really want to change our kitchen. But I had developed a MAJOR problem, which was this. How were Tori and I ever going to invite friends back from our new school when our house looked like something off *DIY SOS*?

Tori had been right to worry about life at secondary school. It was early September, and we'd been at Forrests for exactly one week. It was the scariest place I'd ever been. I was already wondering if I would make it to half-term alive. Life as a new Year Seven in a new school on the other side of town was never going to be easy, but so far it had been worse than impossible. Just as Tori had pointed out four months earlier, none of our friends had come up to Forrests from Castle Hill except Moron, who was more like a hopeful pigeon after crumbs than a friend.

I don't often feel grateful for Tori, which maybe is wrong. She can't help being a nerd. But just now, I was more grateful than I'd ever been in my whole life. All week I'd clung to her like a rubber ring in one of those massive leisure pools with a wave machine. And sharks. She didn't know how much I'd been relying on her, of course. It was more than my life was worth to tell her that.

The downside to us doing the twin thing was that we hadn't spoken to a single other person except for Moron. Consequently we were now in danger of becoming known as the loner weirdos. The other kids had taken one look at the two of us with our boring long brown hair and pale uninteresting skin and lack of pierced anythings, and then another look at the bony, bat-eared Moron hovering around us like the angel of social death, and decided we weren't worth making friends with.

This had to change, or I was going to go MAD. I didn't *want* to hear Tori being sarky and going on about time warps and thermodynamics all day long. I didn't *want* to hear about Moron's terror every time he went into the boys' toilets. I had enough problems of my own. I wanted to laugh and go on sleepovers and pull stupid faces in those glass test tubes we have in science that make your chin go really enormous if you get the angle right. I wanted to find someone cool I could hang out with. And no one cool was going to set foot in a house that looked like a massive brick rat that an even more massive cat is halfway through disembowelling on an even MORE massive sitting-room carpet.

Proper friends won't care about ring marks on the table, I told myself hopefully. Maybe it would be all right. Maybe my magnificent personality would make up for my sister's strange one. Maybe I'd ask someone round next week.

I tried a conversation out for size in my head.

'*Hi. Fancy tea at ours? By the way, we've got two half-grown tigers.*'

I eyed the cubs with a mixture of pride and anxiety. Here was my second problem. I loved the cubs to bits. But having wild animals in your house wasn't exactly *normal*.

Chips was snoring. I watched his back leg twanging through some kind of tiger dream and felt melty all over. This happens a lot when you have baby tigers in your house. You'll have to trust me on this.

'Do you think Chips is dreaming about the jungle?' I said. I liked thinking that the cubs had deep memories of parrots and orchids and mangrove swamps in their blood.

Dad came out of his office, trailing the familiar whiff of hot photographs behind him. When Dad was home, our whole house smelt like one of those photo developing machines you get in Boots.

'Chips left the jungle too young to remember it,' Dad said. He scratched at some angry red insect bites on his furry neck. 'On the other hand, I remember the jungle a bit too well just now. They have mosquitoes the size of budgies in Malaysia.'

'My poor darling,' Mum murmured.

She gave Dad a big lingering kiss through his beard. My folks are well embarrassing with the kissing thing. They were always a nightmare at parents' evenings at Castle Hill – well, this one and only time when Dad was home for parents' evening – and my stomach turns to water every time I think of them coming to a parents' evening at Forrests. Maybe it's because Dad's away so much that Mum needs to kiss him a lot in between.

'It's not the jungle Chips is dreaming about,' said Mum when she (finally) stopped snogging Dad. 'He's dreaming about eating Mr Terry Tanner.'

Terry Tanner, the thief with the private plane and the extremely stupid wife who'd practically starved Chips and Gravy to death, was Mum's pet subject at the moment. After months of phone calls and evidence-gathering, he was finally on trial for smuggling the cubs. We were hoping the verdict would be a big ginormous fat GO TO JAIL. DO NOT PASS GO. DO NOT COLLECT £200.

'Hi, Dad,' Tori said, coming in from the garden where she'd been shovelling yucky tiger mess off the lawn. 'You stink. I hope your pictures are worth it.'

'Morning, Tori,' said Dad politely. 'You stink too. And the pictures *are* worth it, thank you. One of the monkeys I photographed even looks a bit like you.'

I giggled. Tori waggled her fingers under my nose, making me shriek.

'OK,' said Mum. She clapped her hands. 'Now, the cubs need exercise. Rabbit too. You can both take them out.'

Tori grabbed the leads while I poked Chips with my foot. Chips's ears twitched and his tail lashed a bit. Gravy flicked out one of his claws and waved it around lazily.

'Come on, cublings,' I said. 'Walkies.'

There was a thud and a yelp. Mum's coffee slopped into her cereal bowl. Rabbit had jumped up at her favourite word and whacked her head on the table.

# They Don't Eat Dogs

All the houses in our road are set well back, and these big laurel hedges divide everything up. It's pretty quiet. Because we back on to Fernleigh Common, we can take our animals straight out the back gate and exercise them without giving any strangers a heart attack. The local dog-walkers on the common know us and steer clear, although there was one time when Mum had a chimpanzee on a lead and this dachshund freaked out and ran halfway up a tree so his owners had to call the fire brigade to get him down again.

But that doesn't happen very often.

Rabbit didn't need a lead. She waddled out of the back door and down past the pond, sniffing happily at the wet grass. Chips and Gravy on the other hand were so strong that Tori and I almost lost our grips.

'We won't be able to walk them on our own for much longer,' Tori panted as Gravy made a break for the back gate.

'Whoa!' I squealed, hanging on to Chips like mad. He was looking at our pond with a glint in his eye. You know how all you have to do to entertain a baby is give it a bowl of water it can splash around in? Tiger cubs are the same.

I know I saw the cubs every day, but I couldn't believe how *big* they'd become. And they weren't even halfway to how big they were going to be when they were fully grown. Talk about doing your head in. It wouldn't be long before we couldn't keep them any more and they would leave us. I hoped Wild World would take them permanently when that time came, because then at least we could visit.

I didn't want to think about this, so instead I thought about Terry Tanner. I hoped they would send him to prison for life, and snap the wings off his oh-so-private plane while they were at it. It would have been so excellent to be in the courtroom today, with a basket of rotting fishheads to pelt him with when the judge pronounced sentence. I'm creative like that.

'Aren't they sweet?' Tori said, gazing at the cubs as

they gambolled about like something off a Frosties advert.

For my sister, this was like a total love declaration. If she ever gets a boyfriend (which I can't even imagine, to be honest), he better be prepared for lovey-dovey stuff like 'You're OK' and 'Your shirt's not bad'.

'Sweet doesn't really cover it, Tor.' I glanced around like I was breaking out of jail or something. Just in case someone from Forrests happened to come past.

'No one from Forrests is going to come past,' said Tori. She knows me so well that she can read my mind. 'Anyway, I don't know why you're stressing about it. Since when was it a crime to look after tiger cubs?'

'I never said it was a crime,' I said. 'Unless you're Terry Tanner, of course. It's just *not normal*.'

'It was normal when we were at Castle Hill,' Tori said. 'It made us really popular, actually.'

'It's different now,' I said. 'No one at Forrests knows, and until I can work out how to share this information without coming across like a crazy person, I'd like it to stay that way.'

Tori swished on beside me. 'Joe knows,' she said.

'Moron's got even fewer friends than we have,' I pointed out. 'He's not going to blab.'

'You shouldn't call him Moron.'

'He *likes* it,' I told my sister patiently. How many times was I going to have to explain this? 'He's even got it stencilled on his book bag. He says it's empowering, taking a nickname and using it for yourself.'

'Calling yourself by a nickname that a bunch of thick idiots have given you is not empowering,' Tori snorted. 'What's he *thinking* of? Would you do that if you were being picked on? Would you go round telling everyone your name's Weirdo or Zombie or whatever?'

Moron had changed his name on the third day of school. With his head held high, he had announced it to us as we'd been waiting for our shared bus back home. He looked like he'd been crying, so I said straight away I'd call him Moron if he wanted me to and that it was a cool nickname that made him sound well hard. Tori hadn't said a word, frowning instead at the random trainer someone had thrown on the top of the bus shelter like it was completely interesting and not just a knackered old shoe.

'I was a bit surprised when Moron told us to call him Moron,' I admitted. 'But he's the one getting all the grief, so we should support him however we can.

In the name of our shared Castle Hill past.'

Tori still looked unimpressed. But before we could get into a major argument about it, I saw a terrier yipping towards us that knocked the whole Moron question out of my head. It screeched to a halt like something on *Top Gear* when it saw Chips and Gravy. Then it howled and turned round as fast as its teensy legs would carry it. Its owner scooped the dog into her arms and gazed wildly at the cubs. She wasn't local.

'Don't worry,' Tori said. 'They don't eat dogs.'

'Not yet, anyway!' I added, waggling my eyebrows.

It was *supposed* to be a joke, but the lady took off like she had a rocket in her pants.

'I'm never cracking a joke in that kind of situation again,' I said. 'I just end up embarrassing myself.'

'It wouldn't be the first time,' said Tori. 'Ow!'

We headed back home with Tori rubbing a dead arm most of the way. When we came through the gate, the tigers tried to aim for the pond again. But they were tired from their walk and put up only a token fight as Tori and I hauled them onwards.

'They'll have to go in the cages soon,' Tori said, as I sucked the friction burn on my finger from Chips's lead.

I glanced at the cages that Mum had built in our back garden years ago, and stroked Chips's head wistfully. I never liked it when the animals left the house and went outside. Chips stared up at me with his golden tiger gaze. He looked like he had too much black eyeliner on.

'Chips has got such wise eyes,' I said. I pushed open the back door. 'Sometimes I think he knows all the answers in the world. I should take him into school for our next maths test.'

'His paws are too big for the calculator,' Tori pointed out.

It was one of those rare jokes Tori made that were actually funny. We were still laughing as we came inside.

Dad was sitting at the kitchen table. His skin was grey, like it belonged to a dead and rather hairy fish. He was staring at us, but not seeing us at the same time. Talk about creepy. Gravy sniffed him, and Chips did a funny yawny whine.

'Dad?' Tori got to him first. 'Are you OK?'

'Dad?' I squeaked.

Dad's face cleared. 'Hello, troubles,' he said.

The *relief*.

'What happened?' I asked in a high voice.

# Again with the Cool?

Things got worse.

'Terry Tanner can't take our cubs back!' I howled at Tori as we headed down the corridor towards our classroom a week later. Well, I *say* we headed. We were sort of picked up and carried along on a tide of noise and blazers. 'He CAN'T! He and his dim wife starved them, Tor! They were stolen from the wild before they had even opened their eyes and seen their own mother. It's wicked and wrong!'

'Taya, I *know*,' Tori said. 'But he's a free man now. He can try anything he wants.'

Wild World had called to let us know Terry Tanner's new plans before breakfast. Mum went mad. She threw the phone so hard across the kitchen that the back dropped off and we spent five minutes looking for the battery. She then kept trying to phone Dad, even though it must've been about midnight in Colombia. But Dad's phone doesn't even work in the kitchen-towel aisle at the supermarket, so how did she expect it to work out in the jungle?

'He will not HAVE them,' she shouted, giving up and hurling the phone across the kitchen for a second time. 'My babies will not go to *that* man!'

'Wild World will challenge Terry Tanner, Mum,' said Tori as we tried to calm her down. 'They're the ones who are responsible for the cubs. There's nothing we can do. If we fight—'

'If we fight?' Mum looked half mad. '*IF* we fight? We *will* fight!' And then she went off in the stream of Portuguese that Tori and I could barely understand.

Even without the cub situation, I was still having trouble grasping the basic fact that Terry Tanner wasn't going to jail for doing the most evil thing I'd ever heard of. It made no sense.

'I don't understand,' I wailed again. 'Thieves go to prison!'

'Not when they can pay expensive lawyers,' said Tori.

'We WILL fight!' I said, in such a fierce imitation

of Mum that a Year Nine flattened herself against the wall with a terrified look in her eyes as we swept past.

'Great,' Tori said. 'We'll invite Terry Tanner over for a sleepover and some ice cream before pulling his hair and then telling Mum on him. Last time I looked, eleven-year-olds couldn't do much. This is up to Wild World, not us.'

I wanted to strangle my sister. Really seriously strangle her. Didn't she *care*?

As we poured into our classroom, I caught sight of Catherine Turnbull already arguing with Ms Hutson our teacher. With her dyed black hair and her badges and her massive non-regulation school shoes, Cazza Turnbull was something else. We'd only been in the room five seconds, and she was well on the way to her first detention of the day.

A sudden thought struck me like a bullet, pulling me out of my rage in an instant.

'Cazza's parents are lawyers!' I hissed at Tori. 'She's *exactly* the kind of friend we need right now. She'd love the tigers and everything. I just know it. And her mum and dad could advise us on the cubs!'

My sister looked at me like I had a slug hanging out of my nose. 'Cazza Turnbull is trouble,' she said. 'She's already been in detention four times this term and we've only just started week three.'

I peeled my eyes away from Cazza, who was now writing rude words on the window with a marker pen while Ms Hutson's back was turned.

'I'm going to invite her back to ours,' I said.

Tori nearly choked. 'You *what*?'

Ms Hutson was bawling Cazza out again. Cazza stood there with her arms folded, staring at the ceiling and chewing. She was *amazing* with a capital *maze*.

'It's a brilliant idea,' I said firmly. Even if my sister wasn't prepared to fight for our cubs, I was. 'It solves two problems at once. We've been at Forrests for two whole weeks now, and we still know practically nobody. So imagine if we were friends with Cazza!' I said in my most persuasive voice. 'Her folks would help us to keep our cubs, and *everyone* would want to know us. Talk about two birds and one stone!'

'That's a stupid expression,' said Tori. 'Only someone extremely weird wants to throw stones at birds.'

I could hardly breathe as I thought about being friends with Cazza Turnbull. We'd save our tigers. And we'd be *legendary*.

'Detention!' yelled Ms Hutson on the other side of the room.

'Whatever,' said Cazza.

32

While Ms Hutson turned her attention to two boys fighting in the book corner, I stood up from our desk in a fit of bravery and walked over to where Cazza had just flung herself down in a chair at the back of the room.

'Hi, Cazza,' I said. I felt a bit breathless. 'I like your hair. The colour is cool.'

Cazza's eyes travelled very slowly from the tips of my black shoes to the sparkly hairband I'd decided was the riskiest hair accessory I could get away with at school. She didn't say anything.

'Where did you get your shoes?' I ploughed on. 'They are well cool.'

The girls sitting with Cazza sniggered. Cazza didn't blink. She reminded me of a lizard Mum had once.

'I wanted to get some like that only Mum wouldn't let me, which was totally uncool of her.'

I'd said cool too many times. I could hear my voice starting to squeak. Why didn't she answer? I was running out of stuff to say.

'Cool,' I said in despair. *Again* with the cool?

Cazza leaned forward. She had more eyeliner on than Chips. Her friends watched me, snorting like walruses behind their hands.

'Never talk to me again,' she said.

I practically ran back down the room to Tori. A burst of laughter followed me.

'That went well,' Tor observed.

'Shut up,' I muttered.

No one else had noticed my social disaster apart from Moron. He smiled sympathetically from his tidy desk in front of the window. The light coming through the glass made his sticky-out ears red and transparent. I could actually see a bunch of veins in there.

'Are you OK?' he mouthed across the room. Then he gave me this well embarrassing thumbs-up sign. It was nice of him and everything, but just at that minute I wanted to chop both his thumbs off and throw them out of the window.

'There's a MORON in the room,' said Cazza. Her mates laughed.

Moron blushed and lowered his thumbs again. I rested my head on the desk and tried to disappear into the carpet squares under my feet.

'Day eleven at Forrests and the Wild twins are still alive,' Tori intoned as we got bustled down the main corridor at the end of school. Bells shrilled around us; clanging lockers and screeching trainers added to the pain.

'If you're trying to cheer me up, it's not working,' I said as a huge Year Ten pushed me into the hinges on the double doors that got us out into the school car park.

'I'm not trying to cheer *you* up,' Tori said. 'I'm trying to cheer *me* up.'

'Tori? Taya!'

Moron was hurrying towards us, clutching his bag to his chest.

'Can I walk with you?' he said.

'We catch the same bus, don't we?' said Tori.

We started walking down through the car park, on the edge of the main current so we had some kind of control over our feet. Glancing ahead, Moron hesitated. 'Do you mind if we go the back way?' he said.

I stopped, following his gaze to where a bunch of Year Tens were loitering at the gates that led out to the road and our bus stop. Dwight Dingle – the largest, probably the stupidest and definitely the scariest person in the school – was kicking kids at random and guffawing like a gorilla each time he got one.

'Good idea,' I said. I didn't fancy being kicked today.

Tori was still walking.

'Tor?' I called as Moron and I started to head back the way we'd just come. 'We're going the back way.'

'No,' Tori said over her shoulder. 'Our bus stop is just outside the gates.'

'I don't think bus drivers let corpses get on the bus,' I said.

'Go the back way and they've won,' Tori said.

'Sometimes it's OK to let them win,' said Moron in a small voice.

Tori swung round. She pointed hard at me. 'You were the one saying how we couldn't let Terry Tanner bully Wild World and take our cubs, Taya. Now I'm saying it back to you. If you want to fight bullies, you stand up to them. Right?'

I stared at her in dismay. 'It's not quite the same—'

Tor had already turned back round and was marching on.

'You and me could still go the back way,' Moron whispered.

I couldn't do it. I couldn't let my twin sister walk past Dwight Dingle on her own. 'Sorry, Moron,' I said unhappily. 'We have to follow her. It'll be over in two minutes. Honest.'

Moron's face whitened. He clamped his bag to his chest, wet his lips and gave a tight nod. Together we resumed the Walk of Death.

The chant started softly, then rose like an impression of an approaching siren.

'Moron, moron . . . MORON! MORON!'

Don't say anything, I willed Moron as we hurried onwards. There wasn't far to go before we could lose ourselves in the grey-blazered crowd milling about the pavement outside.

'MORON!' the Year Tens sang joyfully.

Dwight Dingle's foot connected with my shin. The shock made me squeal almost more than the pain.

'That's my name, don't wear it out,' Moron said, somehow hopping over Dwight Dingle's foot as it shot out towards him. The bullies practically wet themselves laughing.

'Why do you *do* that, Joe?' Tori said as we made it to the safety of School Road. 'It really truly doesn't help!'

'He's called *Moron*,' I said, limping beside Tori.

Tori threw her hands in the air. 'I don't *want* to call him a moron,' she said.

'We're not calling him *a* moron,' I said doggedly. 'We're calling him *Moron*. It's known as positive action.'

'I am here, you know,' said Moron.

You can't run through fire and come out the other

side still thinking that the person who went through the flames with you isn't your friend. I smiled at Moron, feeling giddy that we'd all made it to the bus stop in one piece.

'We noticed,' I said. 'Listen, do you want to come for tea at ours?'

# 5

# Mother of God, How III?

Moron talked non-stop the whole way back. We heard about how he'd always wanted to come back to ours ever since we'd starting bringing in our animals for Show and Tell at Castle Hill, and how his mum had left when he was nine and his dad was an accountant, and how he'd always wanted a pet but was never allowed one, and how his bedroom had wallpaper with monkeys on. Our brush with Dwight Dingle plus my invitation had opened a flood of words that was going to drown us all.

'Will your mum mind if I call Dad when we get in and let him know where I am?' Moron said breathlessly as we turned into our road from the bus stop. 'I'm only the next road down from you so I can go home whenever, plus he's never home before seven anyway so I just let myself in. Hey, do you remember that time you brought a chameleon to assembly? It was the best thing I've ever seen with its swivelly eyes and mad fingers. And do you remember how it made Zoe McGuigan scream and wet her knickers when it shot out its tongue? It was like a dinosaur, wasn't it? Do you get loads of reptiles? What have you got now? Is it something poisonous?'

I shot a look at Tori. If Moron had gone mental about the chameleon, the tigers were going to send him into orbit.

Although our house is a nightmare, it ticks some fairly normal boxes from the outside. We've got a warped wooden gate, a bumpy driveway, a green front door with a curly lantern thingy that pings on when it's dark, curtains and hanging baskets with dead flowers in and loads of gnarled old apple trees in the front garden. Moron's eyes were out on stalks as he tried to peer through the apple trees and find whatever animals we were hiding.

We had about five seconds before we reached the point where he would be able to see Chips and Gravy at their usual sentry posts in the sitting-room window.

'You're not allergic to cats, are you?' I said.

Moron's eyes grew big. 'Why? What have you got? Lions? Seriously, have you got lions?'

Two seconds. Chips was in position. I could see his furry face through the branches of one of the apple trees closest to the house.

'Not lions, no,' said Tori.

We passed the final apple tree. Chips stood up and leaned his front paws against the sitting-room window. Squashed against the glass, they were the size of dinner plates. His head practically touched the sitting-room ceiling. You couldn't exactly miss him.

Moron's eyes bugged out of his head.

Tori had taken out her keys and was already walking up to the front door.

'You've got a tiger in your sitting room,' Moron said.

It was kind of an obvious thing to say.

'Two actually,' I told him.

Tori unlatched the door and looked over her shoulder. 'You coming in or what?' she said.

'How come they aren't in a cage?' Moron squeaked.

'They're too little,' I explained. 'Young tigers need loads of love and attention, and get lonely if you cage them up. You'll love them, I promise. Come in. We've got custard creams!'

Very slowly, Moron came into the porch.

'The tigers are called Chips and Gravy, by the way,' I said. 'They might give you a bit of a sniff but don't worry about it. They aren't dangerous if you're sensible.'

We came into the hall just as Mum came out of the kitchen. Her eyes had the puffy look of someone who's been crying all day, which she probably had.

'Any more news, Mum?' I asked.

Mum wiped her eyes. 'That man has been contacting Wild World and demanding to know where the cubs are being kept.' She couldn't bring herself to use Terry Tanner's name.

'They didn't tell him, did they?' said Tori in horror.

Mum shook her head. 'They said they are guarding our address and he will never know where they are until this court case is finished.'

It was something, I suppose. I couldn't help shivering though. I would watch out for strangers in our road who were looking too closely at the houses.

'Mum, this is Joe,' said Tori as I put my arm comfortingly around Mum's waist.

'Hello, Mrs Wild,' said Moron, half an eye trained on the sitting-room door like he expected the cubs to come leaping out with their claws flashing in the

42

light of the low-energy bulb in our hall.

He let me drag him into the kitchen. Rabbit looked up from her basket beside the range.

'Cute!' gasped Moron, diverted at once. 'Can I stroke him?'

'It's a her and she's called Rabbit,' Tori said.

Rabbit thumped her fat golden tail at Moron as he bent down to stroke her.

'Thanks for inviting me over,' he said happily, fondling Rabbit's ears. 'I haven't had a playdate since Year Four. And that one didn't have a dog.'

'Or two tigers, I'm guessing,' Tori said.

Chips and Gravy had nosed open the adjoining door to the sitting room and padded into the kitchen to join us. Moron stopped stroking Rabbit and stood really still – well, as still as his shaking knees let him – as Chips sniffed his leg. Chips's head came halfway up Moron's thigh.

'Am I doing this right?' he said nervously. 'Standing still? Should I move? What do I do?'

'You're doing great,' I said. I'd finally located the custard creams and started setting them out on a plate as Tori fetched some juice from the fridge.

Moron had clearly passed some kind of tiger test, because Chips stopped sniffing and rubbed his head on

Moron's legs just like a cat would do.

'I can't believe a tiger just headbutted me!' he gasped, staggering a bit from having Chips put his whole weight behind his head-rub. 'That is so unbelievably cool!' He gazed in wonder at Gravy, who was now sniffing his feet to see if his shoes were worth a nibble.

The phone rang loudly, making Rabbit throw back her head and bark like bonkers. Mum reappeared, tickled Gravy behind the ears and picked up the receiver.

'Hello? Yes, this is Mrs Wild. From Colombia, you say?'

Tori and I beamed at each other. Dad didn't usually get a chance to call us from his assignments, as he was always miles from civilization.

Then the world slipped sideways as Mum sat down very suddenly, her fingers gripping the receiver so tightly that her knuckles started turning white.

'Ill?' she said. 'Mother of God, how ill?'

# 6

# Countdown on a Bomb

They say dying is a bit like a long white corridor. If that's true, I hope the corridor doesn't have square neon lights that buzz over your head like angry insects, or a thousand echoes of a hundred feet all attached to people with misery and pain on their faces. I hope there are no wheeled trolleys that pass you, their passengers wrapped in light-green sheets, drips dangling and clinking and squashy plastic bags pumping nameless stuff through soft rubbery tubes. I'd like my white corridor to have a carpet, and windows with gauzy curtains that flutter like butterfly wings and a view of a meadow not a motorway.

When we turned into Dad's hospital room, I stared at the shrunken person in the hospital bed with tubes coming out of his arms. He was all bones, and his skin was greyer than elephant hide. I glanced around the ward in case we had the wrong bed. There weren't any other beds.

'Is he dead?' Tori asked, as blunt as a rolling pin.

I gave a half-hiccup and covered my mouth with my hand.

'No,' said the big-nosed doctor standing beside the thing that was Dad. 'He is in a coma. But we're hopeful that he will come round very soon. The Colombian doctors recognized the problem as soon as they saw it. They gave him the right drugs and put him straight on a plane back home. Their actions probably saved his life.'

'What *is* the problem?' Tori asked. She looked even whiter than Mum.

'Type one diabetes,' Doctor Nose told us.

'One of the kids at Castle Hill had diabetes,' I said. 'It didn't put *him* in a coma. Why's my dad in a coma?'

'It's unusual in adults,' Doctor Nose explained, 'and very dangerous if left untreated. Often, an undiagnosed case can result in death.'

*Cheers, doc*, I thought. *That's really made me feel groovy*. I had a flash memory of Dad going weird in the kitchen the day we heard Terry Tanner wasn't going to jail. Had that been the start? And he'd been looking so tired . . .

'He will get better,' said Mum, when Doctor Nose finished explaining Dad's condition. She was squeezing my hand so hard that I was starting to lose all feeling in my fingers. I noticed she was doing the same to Tori on the other side. 'He will wake up.'

'He *should* wake up,' corrected Doctor Nose. 'But he will always have diabetes. Diabetes is incurable.'

I was liking Doctor Nose less and less. What was with the 'should' part? And the negative stuff? Why couldn't he tell us some good news?

'The good news is that with the right medication, your father will be able to live a normal life,' said the doctor. 'He will have to make a lot of adjustments to his lifestyle and his diet, and he will be on medication for the rest of his life. But provided he does all that, he won't be in a wheelchair, or bedbound.'

There, I thought with relief. Not that bad at all. With some drugs and a change of diet, Dad would be back to normal in no time.

'Of course, we need him to wake up first,' the doctor added.

Well, that sent us all straight back into the pit. Dad had to wake up. He *had* to. My heart, already breaking from our horrible day, broke that little bit more. Fate was as bad as Dwight Dingle. Not content with trying to take our cubs away, now it had Dad in its slimy fingers as well.

You can't leave young tigers alone in a house for more than five minutes, by the way. They get super-anxious and rip up the furniture. When we got back from the hospital, our neighbour Rob was standing at the kitchen door with his hands on Chips's and Gravy's heads while the cubs tried to lick his knees. He looked pleased that we were back. So did the cubs, who made their special *vuvuvuv* noise at us, the one they use to say hello when they haven't seen us for a bit.

Mum knelt down and buried her face in the cubs' fur. Tori's face was stony, and I don't know what I looked like. Half mad probably, with tears and bogeys dropping off the end of my nose.

'Everything – er, all right then?' said Rob.

Plainly, with Mum almost lying full-length on the floor, everything was very much not all right.

'Not really,' said Tori, fixing him with serious eyes. 'But Dad's not dead.'

She'd summed up our entire awful day in just six words. No soppy stuff, no twiddly bits. Just the bald facts. I admired her for it. It would have taken me at least a thousand.

'Sorry,' said Rob helplessly. 'I mean, great. Sorry, but great. I'll er – I'll be off then. Doris needs her tea.'

He disappeared back to Doris his very un-tiger-ish dog. Tori silently put the kettle on and I helped Mum on to one of the kitchen chairs and held her hand for a bit.

As the kettle reached its mournful train-whistle stage, the phone rang. I left Mum with both the cubs resting their heads on her knees and went to answer it.

'Is that Tori or Taya?'

'It's Taya, Moron,' I said, sinking into the sofa.

'You just got back then? Is everything OK?'

I tried really hard to be like Tori. 'Not really, but Dad's not dead at least, so that's something. He looked it, though. You never saw so many tubes in your life and there's this horrible screen by his bed that blips at you like the countdown on a bomb and—' I stopped myself, took a deep breath. 'Look, can we talk at school tomorrow? It's been a really long day.'

'Will you be at school?' said Moron.

'Mum said we have to go in,' I said. 'There's no point brooding around here. There's nothing we can do.'

'For real?'

He sounded so relieved that we would be there tomorrow that I asked, 'Did Dwight Dingle get you today?'

'Yes,' Moron said sadly.

'Did you do your "That's my name, don't wear it out" thing?' I checked.

Moron sounded even gloomier. 'Yes.'

Moron's attempt at positive action really wasn't working. I felt a swell of anger. Who did Dwight Dingle think he was, with his spotty chin and swinging feet? 'Bus stop tomorrow, usual time?' I said.

'OK,' said Moron. 'And you don't have to talk about your dad if you don't want to,' he added unexpectedly. 'But if you do want to talk about him, I'll listen. And if you want to talk about other stuff I'll listen to that too. Especially if you want to talk about the tigers. I had a great time yesterday, and it didn't matter about not having the pizza.'

'Thanks,' I said.

I put the receiver down, thinking how Moron was full of surprises. It wasn't fair he got so picked on. He was solid, once you got past his sticking-out ears and habit of putting his thumbs up at embarrassing moments.

I was glad we had.

# 7

# But We Don't Have Monkeys in Surrey

It was a very long week. Each day Tori and I shook off the horrors of school and said goodbye to Moron at our bus stop and hurried home with our hearts in our mouths to see if Mum had any news on Dad. Each day she greeted us at the door with a white face and the same big bruised-looking pouches under her eyes, which spelled out another day of antiseptic nothingness at the hospital. I think the tigers were the only things that stopped Mum from flipping out completely.

With Wild World on the phone most days updating Mum on Terry Tanner's latest move, even thinking about the tigers wasn't exactly unstressful. Every time I saw someone unfamiliar in our road, I got jumpy.

What if he found us? We didn't exactly live far away from the safari park. What if he just broke into the house one day and took them away?

By Friday, Tori and I were so fed up we were on the verge of feeding each other to Sufi, Mum's corn snake. We sat stiffly together in the kitchen after school, grooming Chips and Gravy while they slept and winkling out any ticks we could find before the cubs woke up and pushed us over. As I worked, I tried not to think about the image from the hospital of the tubes going up Dad's poor old nose and the needles in his arms. *Is Dad dead? Is Dad dead?* Tori's question took up a bony rhythm in my head and blocked out everything else.

'Listen,' we both said at the same time.

'You first,' said Tori.

I laid down my brush. 'We have to stop fighting,' I said. 'It's not good for Mum. It's not helping Dad either.'

'I know,' said Tori. 'I think it's because I'm scared.'

What?

*I* was the scaredy-cat in this house. I screeched at spiders and couldn't watch any of Tor's *Doctor Who* videos without a large cushion to hide behind and a bar of chocolate for the shock.

'*You're* scared?' I said.

Tor shrugged. 'It happens.'

'What's your scariest thing?' I asked. I braced myself for a sarcastic answer.

'Depends,' Tor said. She kept brushing Chips. 'I think about what might happen if Dad doesn't wake up, and that's the scariest thing. The next moment I think about losing our cubs and then *that's* the scariest thing. School is so awful that I don't really know where to start.'

'But you're all confident at school!' I said, still in shock that my sister was, apparently, being entirely serious.

'No way,' Tor said. 'You're the confident one.'

'You're the one who makes us all walk past Dwight Dingle every day!' I protested.

'That's easy,' Tori said. 'The Doctor stands up to aliens all the time, and Dwight Dingle doesn't have death-ray eyes or a load of poisonous tentacles. Making friends is way harder. You tried to make friends with Cazza, didn't you?'

I grimaced. 'I fell flat on my face, if you remember.'

'But you tried,' Tori said. 'I envy that.'

This was by far the strangest thing Tori had ever said to me.

'Hello?' I patted the air around me like I was in a weird new dimension. 'This isn't the way we are. Have we fallen through a slughole or something?'

'Wormhole,' said Tor.

I looked warily at her.

'Don't look at me like that, Taya,' Tori said, 'or I'll laugh, and I'm really really trying not to.'

We gazed at each other like we'd just got in a cage with a new and completely unexpected alien species.

'Joe calling himself Moron,' I said at last, busying myself with checking Gravy's big squashy paw pads for cuts and splinters. 'It's a terrible idea, isn't it?'

'Yes,' said Tori.

'I'll stop calling him Moron,' I said. 'From Monday, I'll call him Joe.'

'Good idea,' my sister said.

'*Vuvuvuv*,' said Gravy, lifting his head sleepily from my lap.

On Saturday morning, the miracle occurred and Dad woke up. I'm glad there were no police cars watching the motorway because Mum drove us to the hospital like a total loony.

'Hello, troubles,' Dad said in a croaky voice, and

Tori and I fought like puppies to cuddle him across the bed. 'You're a gorgeous sight, both of you.'

'You're not,' said Tori. 'You look horrible.'

Dad gave a tired laugh. On the other side of the bed, Mum held his hand and stroked his fingers one by one.

Doctor Nose checked off something on his clipboard. 'A good recovery,' he said, looking up. 'Took a while, though. You had us worried, Mr Wild.'

He sounded quite pleased about this.

'So, doc,' said Dad. 'What happens now?' He spoke slowly, as if moving his mouth was as hard as climbing a mountain.

After rambling on for a bit, Doctor Nose finally said something that I understood.

'You were two days away from the nearest town in Colombia, and nearly died before a doctor could treat you. While you learn to manage your condition I would strongly advise you not to travel to such far-flung places. For the foreseeable future, it would be best to find work closer to home.'

It took a few seconds for this to sink in. Then I said the first thing that came into my head.

'But we don't have monkeys in Surrey!'

We didn't have lyre birds or meerkats or gazelles

either. What was Dad going to photograph round here? Labradors?

'All I can do is offer my advice,' said Doctor Nose. 'And that's it.'

Mum burst into tears. Taking Dad's hand, she started gabbling at him in Portuguese. Dad began nodding and making soothing noises.

'You are telling him to stay at home, aren't you Mum?' Tori checked.

We understand Portuguese, and we can chat with the rellies if we have to. But when Mum gets overexcited, her words get mushed up together in a big consonant soup without any vowels at all. How Dad understands her beats me. That's love, I guess.

'Of *course* I am telling him to stay,' Mum said, wiping her eyes. 'And of *course* he agrees. He won't leave us ever again.'

'I don't know which would kill me first,' Dad said weakly. 'The diabetes or my life insurance.'

I didn't know what to feel. Part of me was awash with the deepest, most wonderful relief. Dad was awake and Dad was staying! In England! For ever! He could manage the diabetes with drugs and diet, Doctor Nose had said. And we could look after him and maybe he'd even shave his beard off if I asked him nicely. It would be lovely having him at home. Strange, but lovely.

The rest of me couldn't help wondering how a wildlife photographer was going to make a living stuck in Surrey.

'What are you going to do instead?' asked Tori, echoing my thoughts.

Dad was quiet for a minute. 'I've got no idea,' he said at last.

And then he fell asleep and we tiptoed out and I did this totally embarrassing skid on a shiny patch of floor and this boy aged about fifteen really laughed for ages down the corridor with it echoing back at me for what felt like my entire life.

Dad was to stay in hospital for another week as he recovered a bit more and learned how to give himself insulin injections. I spent most of the journey back to Fernleigh making suggestions about what he could do now he couldn't fly round the world doing double-page spreads on spitting cobras for *National Geographic*. I was remembering a bit too well what Mum had said when we were having the Conversation, about Dad's job paying for our house.

'Please, Taya darling.' Mum wearily put her keys down on the hall table and put two slim brown hands over her ears. 'I can't think about this right now or I will go mad.'

'Maybe Dad could be Wild World's official photographer,' I suggested, as Rob scurried back home to Doris and the tigers fussed around us like they hadn't seen us for a million years. 'I don't know if they have one already but I'm sure he'd be brilliant at it. He knows all the best angles on lions and—'

'Come on, Taya,' said Tori loudly. 'We've got homework.'

I protested, but Tori dragged me up the stairs. For such a pune, Tor's well strong. Chips and Gravy padded up the stairs after us like two stripy shadows. I could feel Gravy's cold nose pressing against my leg.

'We have to think of *something*!' I insisted as Tori pushed me across the ink splodge on the landing carpet and up the spiral stairs to our bedroom at the top of the house. 'You must see how important it is!'

'You don't know when to stop, do you?' Tori said.

'If we don't come up with a plan, we'll have to leave this house and go and live in a *flat*,' I said in a voice of doom, cuddling Chips's massive head in my arms while trying to stay out of his tongue's way. 'Chips and Gravy, not to mention Rabbit and Fernando and Sufi, all the other animals Mum gets – they can't live in a flat, Tor.

Can you picture us all in the lift?'

Tori sat down on her bed. To my shock, I realized that my sister was crying. All my anger went *poof* like one of those mushrooms.

'I'm sorry,' I said in horror, sitting next to my twin on the Doctor's duvet legs and cautiously putting my arms round her. We didn't hug much. 'I'm an idiot.'

'Yes, you are,' Tori said in a bogey-soaked voice.

'It's more important that we stay calm for Mum, isn't it?' I said humbly. 'And Dad. They'll be worried too. So we mustn't be worried, right? 'Cos then *they'll* be worried that *we're* worried and they've got more important things to worry about right now. Right?'

Tori did a big sigh. She sounded like when Rabbit sighs at the sight of our Sunday roast. And then Gravy pounced on my foot, which kind of changed the subject.

# 8

# The Spirit of the Doctor

Dad came home. Mum had made a big effort to get the house looking nice for him. Tori and I had cleaned Fernando and Sufi's cages until they gleamed, groomed Rabbit and tied two yellow ribbons round Chips's and Gravy's necks. We'd washed the floors and we'd hoovered. The beds all had clean sheets on and there wasn't a single poo on the back lawn.

'What's this, the Hilton?' Dad said when Mum helped him through the front door.

'We actually polished the kitchen floor,' I told him. 'It took ages and no one's allowed to walk on it now.' Dad looked at me.

'So how do we reach the kettle?' he asked. 'Float?'

'Socks,' I explained. 'Take your boots off, Dad.

Let's get you comfy.'

With Tori on one side and me on the other, we propelled Dad through the sitting-room door and settled him down on our huge grey sofa with its mixture of patchwork cushions and odd decorative splat of jam off a piece of morning toast.

'What do you want?' Tori asked.

'A cup of tea?' I said. 'We've got a new box of Earl Grey.'

Tori turned on the telly. 'BBC?' she said.

'Hot-water bottle?' I called from the adjoining kitchen/sitting-room door.

'This really *is* the Hilton,' said Dad, smiling ever so slightly. 'Are you room service? What have you done with my daughters?'

Tori gets her sense of humour from Dad, needless to say.

Chips and Gravy had followed us all into the sitting room. Now they jumped on to the sofa next to Dad while Mum stroked his head like he was one of the cubs. Gravy started biting Dad's elbow while Chips gave him a good sniff. They hadn't seen him for a while, and I think tigers have quite short memories.

'I've got two hot-water bottles right here,' Dad said. 'But a cup of tea would be great. Two sugars.'

'You're not allowed sugar in your tea, remember?' I said. 'We have to measure your glucose levels every day and sugar will send you off the scale. We've even got a gadget to measure you so you can't pretend.' I waved our new blood glucose meter at Dad.

'You've got an appointment with the dietician on Monday too,' Tori added, 'and they'll know if you cheat.'

'Just one lump?' Dad wheedled. 'I've been dying for a decent cup of tea all week. Hospital tea tastes like washing-up water.'

'You have sugar, I will divorce you,' said Mum with a blazing look in her eyes that made me wonder if she actually meant it.

'Scrap that bit about the Hilton,' Dad said grumpily.

'MORON!' Dwight Dingle shouted as he blundered on to the bus on Monday morning with his gorilla pack.

'That's my name, don't wear it out!' said Joe doggedly as he tried to blend in with the puke-coloured bus seats. When you're as pale as a slice of roast chicken, this is not possible to do.

I felt for him. I really did. It was no fun being called

a moron in front of a busload of other kids, most of whom found it even funnier than Dwight Dingle did. Why I ever thought his idea of calling *himself* Moron was a good one, I'll never know.

'Dad's back from hospital,' I told him, to change the subject.

He gave me a trembly smile. 'Cool. He's OK then?'

'Kind of.'

I told him the situation. He spotted the flaw at once.

'So what job's he going to do instead?'

Tori and I had spent most of the weekend working on a solution to this exact problem. The Wild World safari park didn't need a photographer, and although Dad had rung up all his contacts on the magazines he worked for, no one had offered him an office job. As Tori had put it last night, in her usual direct way: a wildlife photographer who couldn't travel was basically stuffed.

'We don't know, Joe,' I said.

'Moron,' he corrected, looking surprised that I'd forgotten.

'I can't call you that any more,' I said. I spread my hands apologetically. 'I shouldn't have done it to start with. You're Joe from now on, OK?'

64

Joe seemed to accept this. In fact, he looked quite relieved. He thought a bit, staring at his large hands.

'Will you lose your house and your animals?' he said after a minute.

'Blimey,' I said, blinking. 'I thought Tori was direct.'

Joe looked intent. 'Will you?'

'No,' I said firmly. I had no idea how we could change any of the bad stuff that was happening, but saying 'No' felt like the first step.

'Dad can still point a camera at stuff and click,' Tori said. 'The doctor's just told him to find a job in England for a while instead of on the Equator.'

'But what if there's no job?'

I'd had enough of this whole negative vibe. 'There'll *be* a job,' I said.

'But what if there isn't a job round *here*?' Joe suddenly sounded desperate. 'You'll leave Fernleigh!'

The tips of his large ears had turned red and he was gripping his book bag like it was a lifebelt. And I realized that he maybe wasn't the ideal person to have followed us from Castle Hill and he definitely wasn't cool but he *was* our friend and he needed us. It was a bit of a revelation, to be honest. I'd been feeling like my head was in a paper bag and I couldn't see where I was going. But no more. Taya Wild was on the case.

'We aren't going anywhere,' I said, banging my hand down on the ripped armrest. 'We'll think of something. Someone's bound to need a wildlife photographer round here. Right?'

Joe gripped his book bag tighter.

'And Tori and I will get jobs,' I went on, improvising as I went. 'There's loads of things we can do. Wash cars. Mow lawns.'

Tori stopped chewing the end of her plait and looked up. Something was glimmering in her eyes. I think it was hope. 'What about deliveries?' she said. 'Mrs Mason at number ten's always shopping in CostQuik down the road and she can hardly walk and she's not the only one.'

'Exactly!' I said, feeling excited all of a sudden.

Joe looked happier. 'I can always come over and help with the animals if you and your parents have to be out at work at the same time,' he said.

'Well well, if it isn't the Twit Twins and their little moron friend.'

I felt my heart sink into my stomach, roll down my leg and plop into the toe of one of my socks. Cazza was swinging on the yellow holding post in front of us. Standing with her were her mates, Heather Cashman and Carrie Taylor. If I had to choose between a fight

66

with Cash 'n' Carrie and a bite from Gravy, I'd choose Gravy. And he's got seriously massive teeth.

'Don't call him Moron,' said Tori.

I looked sideways at my sister. She was using her dangerous voice.

Cazza grinned. 'He likes it,' she said. 'Don't you, Moron?'

Joe didn't say anything.

'Cazza?' said Tori. 'Did you know me and Taya have got two pet tigers?'

Whatever I'd been expecting, it wasn't that. What was Tori doing? I'd specifically told her NOT to mention our animals to anyone at school, and here she was, chucking it into the conversation like bait into a pit of crocodiles!

Cazza gawped, then recovered. 'You have not,' she said.

'Joe's seen them,' Tori continued. 'Haven't you, Joe?'

Joe nodded, his eyes wide and frightened.

'And the thing is,' Tori continued, standing up, 'I'm thinking of bringing them into school next week. Would you like that?'

'You aren't just weird,' said Cazza after a moment. 'You're totally nuts.'

'They aren't dangerous if you treat them right,' said

Tori, like Cazza hadn't said anything at all. She leaned a little closer so her nose was practically touching Cazza's. 'But they hate the smell of *bullies*.'

Cash 'n' Carrie glanced from Cazza to Tori and back again as Cazza tried to think of something to say back. She gave up and kicked the holding post instead, mouthing 'Weirdos!' at us and heading for the back of the bus with her mates trailing after her.

'Brilliant, Tori,' said Joe.

'Yes,' I said in amazement.

My twin muttered something furious, sat down and went back to chewing her hair. She had clearly been moved by the spirit of the Doctor.

I slunk a glance down the bus at Cazza. She narrowed her eyes at me like Gravy does when he's about to pounce. Any optimism I was feeling that Tori had maybe done the right thing mentioning the tigers faded on the spot. Now all I could see was how our lives at Forrests were about to get much, *much* worse.

If I thought too hard about this, I knew I would cry. So I thought about the other problem in our lives instead. How were we going to earn enough money to keep our house and make sure our lives stayed the same?

There had to be a way.

# Clang of Doom

It wasn't much of a week.

Dwight Dingle was as bad as ever and got my shins twice. Unsure whether Tori'd been winding her up about the tigers, Cazza chose the safe option and ignored us, apart from calling us weirdos every once in a while. It wasn't quite what I'd hoped for. Dreams of making friends with the coolest girl in Year Seven still hung on my horizon like an exhausted seagull at the end of a very long day of scrounging chips. But being ignored wins over being beaten up every time. I'd work on the friendship later. There was plenty of time.

The only half-decent thing to come out of the week was Joe's new attitude towards the bullies. He'd started ignoring shouts of 'MORON!' instead of adopting his positive action approach, much to the Year Tens' disappointment.

When we got home on Friday, Dad called us in to the sitting room. He was by the window with a load of papers in his hand, looking like Ms Hutson when she's about to take the register. His beard was worse than ever. Mum stood beside him. Tori and I sat on the sofa, avoiding the holey bit where the cubs had snacked on the foam lining. Gratefully, I cuddled Chips as he butted his warm head under my chin. I felt like I needed to hold on to something.

Dad did his special throat-clearing noise, the one that sounds like a gorilla coughing in a misty jungle. 'I'm sorry about this, loves,' he said.

It wasn't a good start. I felt Tori's hand sneak into mine and squeeze it. I went briefly into shock. What with our conversation about both feeling scared the other day and now this, we were in danger of becoming, like, close.

'Our lives need to change, as you know,' Dad said. 'More than I would have liked. I have found some local work, but as you can imagine there's not much in the way of elephant portraits in Fernleigh.'

Mum laughed. It sounded like she was swallowing a crisp sideways.

'So, the basic fact is . . .' Dad stopped, stared at his papers, started again. 'The basic fact,' he said again, 'is that we need to change a few things round here or . . .' He swallowed. 'Or we will lose our house.'

This was it. The conversation I'd been dreading for weeks.

Although I'd thought about losing our house a lot since we'd learned that Dad should stay closer to home for a while, hearing him actually say it was awful. It was like looking at a picture of a roaring dinosaur that suddenly jumps off the page and tries to kill you for real. We were going to *lose our house*. The house we'd been in all our lives, with its falling-down ceilings and wobbly banisters, rotten old apple trees and ink-splodged carpet. I pictured us walking around Fernleigh Common calling, 'House? HOUSE! Come back! Where are you?', like we used to do with Rabbit back when she had the energy to disappear in search of rabbits in the undergrowth.

Mum went and stood with Dad. 'I have to go out and find a job too,' she said. 'Your father's income with local work won't be enough without an income from me as well.'

71

'You've got an income,' I objected. 'Looking after the animals.'

'It doesn't pay enough,' Mum said quietly.

'If you're out at work,' Tori said, looking down at the cubs nestled between us, 'who's going to look after Chips and Gravy?'

There was a silence that made me think of the hole in the sofa. Into my head came a mewling box, tied up with ribbons.

'I have called Wild World and explained our situation,' said Mum hopelessly. 'They are very sorry to hear about our difficulties, but their priority is the tigers. They have agreed to take the cubs back and find a different foster carer.'

For a moment, I thought perhaps Mum had been talking Portuguese and I hadn't understood. Had she really just said we were going to lose the cubs?

'No,' I said. It was the only word I could find inside my muddled head.

Mum pleated her T-shirt between her fingers. 'And it may be that . . . that man will take the cubs back after all. Wild World say that he is applying for a Dangerous Wild Animals licence now.'

I felt like Dwight Dingle had just sunk a punch into my stomach.

'Not Terry Tanner. Not him!' I gasped. 'What about other safari parks? Zoos? Someone else must be out there. I—'

'If Tanner gets the cubs, he'll look after them,' Dad interrupted in a tight voice. 'He'll be watched so closely that he won't be able to pop to Tesco without an animal welfare officer breathing down his neck. They'll be fine without us.'

Tori sat as still as a heron.

'But *we* won't be fine!' I burst out in horror. 'We can't lose them! We can't let *him* have them! Mum, you don't want that, do you? Do you?'

Mum passed her hand over her face. 'Of course not,' she said. 'But we can't keep the animals *and* the house. And we need to think of you girls.'

'We'll move!' I said wildly.

'It's not as simple as that,' Dad said.

'Tori and I will get jobs!' I tumbled on. 'We'll . . . we'll . . .'

'I'm sorry, Taya. We've made our decision,' said Dad. 'Wild World will come and take the cubs on Wednesday.'

He dropped his papers on the coffee table and walked out of the sitting room. Mum ran after him.

BONG.

I'd never heard a real Clang of Doom before. I mean, I've heard a few dings and dongs, like over Dad's diabetes and the whole Cazza business. But here was the real deal, ringing in my ears.

# 10

## Tigers Can't Smile

Going back to school after half-term was strange. I couldn't get over how everything outside our house was exactly the same even though Tori and I had been turned inside out like socks. Why hadn't the world tipped over?

Joe'd been on holiday to Tenerife with his dad during half-term, so he'd missed the latest drama. He could tell something was majorly wrong though. He kept looking at us with these big worried eyes, waiting for us to explain, and jabbing his bony thumbs at the sky to cheer us up. The only good part of the day was when Heather Cashman, Cazza's henchwoman, said 'All right?' to me outside the toilets. I think maybe she believed what Tori'd said on the bus about the tigers, but didn't dare to double-check in case she made a total idiot of herself. Pet tigers in Surrey are unlikely, after all.

At the end of the day, we all ploughed past the school gates towards the bus stop. Dwight Dingle had got bored of hanging around the gates every single day of term, and had started limiting himself to twice a week. So three times a week we quite enjoyed walking together, out of the stuffy sock-smelling corridor and into the car park. Even better, today there was a rumour that Dwight Dingle was on detention for setting fire to the chemistry lab, so he wouldn't be on the bus either. On days like this, school felt almost bearable, if you took away the tarmac and the graffiti and the litter that swirled almost as thickly around our ankles as the leaves that fell from Forrests's one and only tree.

'Why call a school Forrests when it's only got one tree?' Joe said as we got on the bus.

'There was probably a primeval jungle here once,' Tori said. 'With Dwight Dingle's relatives swinging from the trees.'

It was the most she'd said all day. Joe looked encouraged. 'Can I come back to yours?' he said hopefully. 'It feels like ages since I saw the cubs and Dad's in London again this week. So that means he doesn't get home till past nine most evenings. Unless . . .' He trailed off, leaving a nice fat gap for us to start explaining why we'd been so weird all day.

'Sure,' said Tori, ignoring the gap. Joe was too pleased at the invitation to push his luck.

We stayed quiet all the way through town and up the hill. It was only when we were approaching our stop that it occurred to me how empty our house would be when the tigers left and Mum went out to work. We'd be just like Joe.

'Joe,' I said as we got off the bus. 'Do you ever get lonely?'

'I've always been lonely,' said Joe. 'I don't really notice it most of the time.'

'Tell your dad to do a different job,' advised Tori.

'I suggested animal-fostering to him the other day,' Joe said. 'But he says he likes being an accountant.'

We came through the door. Joe chucked his coat over our banister in one throw. He'd had a lot of practice, being round at ours at least twice a week before half-term.

'Phew,' he said as Chips jumped up at him to say hello. Chips was so big now he could actually put his paws on Moron's shoulders. 'Your breath stinks, Chips.'

'He ate his last toothbrush weeks ago,' said Tori.

Joe stopped rubbing Chips's head. 'You actually brush their *teeth*?'

He was even more gullible than me.

'Joke,' Tori and I both said patiently.

In the kitchen, Dad was staring at a pile of bank statements and other bits of paper scattered around him on the table. Everything was covered with coffee-mug marks. He hardly noticed as we slipped through and out the back door with Joe and the cubs. Rabbit did though, and struggled out of her basket to follow us.

Mum was at the vegetable patch, weeding like a mad person. She'd been weeding pretty much non-stop since Dad's awful little speech in the sitting room, in between visiting her agent in search of modelling work and coming home again in an even worse mood than before.

'Any work for your dad yet?' Joe asked in a low voice as we threw sticks for Rabbit and the cubs to chase.

'He's started doing a few school photos,' said Tori, 'but it's not enough.'

I took a deep breath. 'Things got worse over half-term,' I said. 'The cubs are leaving on Wednesday.'

Joe's jaw dropped open. 'What?'

'Wild World is taking them back and finding another foster carer,' Tori told him. 'Mum has to find work as well now. Outside the house, I mean.'

'That's terrible,' said Joe in horror. 'Will that Terry Tanner get them now?'

Even hearing Terry Tanner's name made me feel sick. 'We don't know,' I said thickly, my own voice filling with tears. 'The only thing that can put everything right now is a magic wand and we don't have one.'

It still didn't seem real. I had tried telling myself that without the tigers we could perhaps paint the kitchen and get a new carpet, but it wasn't helping. It was like someone was pulling my heart out of my chest extremely slowly. Sometimes I wished they would just yank it out and the cubs would go and it would all be over. Other times I felt sick with misery that they were slipping through our fingers like sand and no matter how tightly we closed our fingers the grains were still getting through.

Chips made a fantastic flying leap through the air after a stick that Joe had thrown. He landed in the middle of the vegetable patch, making Mum launch into a massive arm-waving, Portuguese-roaring tornado. The cubs fled to a safe distance, the glossy stripes around their golden bodies shining like black ribbons.

'You should put the tigers on YouTube,' said Joe. 'I watch hilarious animal clips on that all the time.'

The breath flew out of me as everything went into slow motion. Joe's school trousers were too short for his long legs and flapped above his gigantic black trainers. They reminded me of sails on the two skinny masts of a yacht. Yet somehow he suddenly looked like the coolest person in the entire universe.

'*Animal modelling*,' I breathed. 'Joe Morton, you're a genius!'

Joe looked astonished. 'I am?'

I tore inside like a hurricane about to miss the bus.

'Dad, can we borrow one of your cameras?' I said breathlessly. 'One with a video mode?'

Dad looked up from the kitchen table. 'What for?'

The light outside was fading, so we didn't have a lot of time. But I knew this much. A film of the tigers would look unbelievable in the sunset, especially if I could get in the shine from the garden pond too.

'Quickly!' I panted.

Dad half stood, infected by my excitement. 'Take one from the second drawer in my desk,' he called after me as I swerved round the range and past the kitchen table and out into the hall with Joe and Tori following me like those whooshy bits that come out of Peter Pan's feet.

'Second drawer, second drawer . . .'

I hunted through Dad's desk. There were old rolls of film, and neatly filed negatives, lenses and tripod legs, computer disks and envelopes and endless yellow Post-its stuck everywhere. I leaned right into the depths of the second drawer and carefully took out a camera. Then I held it up, hoping that I looked a bit like the Statue of Liberty.

'Our future,' I said impressively.

'You've got a Post-it on your bum,' said Tori.

I ignored this. 'The light'll go any minute,' I said, checking the camera had enough battery power and rushing back past Joe and Tori as they hung around in the doorway. 'The cubs haven't had their tea yet, have they? Go and get some meat, Tor. We'll use it as bait.'

'We'll give them a bit each time they smile for the camera,' Tori said.

'Tigers can't smile,' Joe said doubtfully.

'JOKE!' I shouted, rushing back through the kitchen.

The sun was a glowing basketball, hovering over the treetops of Fernleigh Common and turning everything a gorgeous Lucozade colour.

'Joe, you take Chips down there,' I said, pointing to the far side of the pond. 'I'll hold Gravy.'

Joe obediently dragged Chips down the garden. I took a handful of Gravy's warm scruff. When Tori appeared with the meat, everything was going to kick off BIG time.

'I'm not going to ask,' said Dad from the back door. Mum stood up by the vegetable patch to watch. 'Should I ask?'

'Tor!' I yelled, bracing myself as Gravy wriggled. The camera was in danger of slipping out of my hand. 'Where's the beef?'

Tori appeared beside Dad, holding two buckets of meat scraps. At the bottom of the garden, Chips nearly pulled Joe's arm off. Gravy did the same with me. If I hadn't already slung Dad's camera round my neck it would have shot off and away into the air like the sticks we'd been throwing. Rabbit waddled outside to see what all the fuss was about. She put her nose into the meat buckets and Tori shooed her away.

'Get the buckets in between the cubs!' I shouted at Tori, struggling to hold Gravy still.

Tori ran down the garden with the buckets. That was when I knew she agreed with me that this was the answer to *everything*. Tori only ran when she really wanted to. She put the buckets on the path in between the tigers and stepped back.

'Rabbit, no!'

Tori started forward again as Rabbit lumbered towards the buckets. Chips was practically choking himself with excitement, and had actually pulled Joe on to his knees.

'Leave Rabbit,' I panted, wrestling to hold the camera with one hand and Gravy with the other. 'I can't hold Gravy much longer. Everyone ready? GO!'

I struggled to whip the camera into position and press the video button as the tigers shot away at the same time. They bore down on the buckets of meat in the middle of the path like those jousting knights you see at Leeds Castle.

Rabbit was tilting her head to get her jaws into one of the buckets. She totally failed to notice the two stripy express trains heading towards her. Filming like mad, I crept forward. Once I worked out how to put this film on YouTube with Joe's help, Chips and Gravy were going to be *famous*. And then loads of requests for filming them would flood in and everything would be safe.

'Get out of the way, Rabbit!' Dad roared. 'Do you

want to be a dog sandwich?'

Rabbit looked up just in time. She leaped about ten feet into the air. The tigers collided underneath her, so she ended up straddling them like a double tiger rodeo. She clung on stupidly as Chips and Gravy dug their heads deep into their buckets, then slid off sideways. Tori was helpless with laughter on the far side of the path. I moved closer. This was better than I could have hoped. This was a work of genius. This would be snapped up by—

'Taya, LOOK OUT!'

I never got as far as thinking exactly who my film was going to be snapped up by, because my foot suddenly met thin air. I toppled forward. Somehow I still had the tigers in focus. But the shock of the freezing-cold pond changed all that.

# 11

## Frying Eggs in High Heels

As Mum mopped me with a towel and tucked my sopping trainers into the bottom oven of the range to dry, Joe was doing his best not to laugh. Which is more than I can say for my sister.

'We should have filmed you, not the tigers,' Tori wailed, still doubled over by the back door. 'That was the funniest thing I've ever seen.'

'Don't laugh, Tori,' Mum sighed. 'It's not kind.'

'Sorry,' said Tori, before dissolving again.

'Did I ruin your camera, Dad?' I sniffed.

Dad was staring out of the window. He hadn't moved since I'd come dripping through the back door. He looked like someone had hit him over the head.

'Dad?' I said again.

Dad moved like a ghost, out of the kitchen and into the hall. I heard him go into his study and shut the door.

I don't think I've ever felt so bad in my life. I wanted to crawl into the bottom oven of the range and shrivel up beside my trainers. Dad loved his cameras like I loved the cubs. And even though the cameras in the second drawer weren't his best ones, they were still expensive. Somehow my perfect plan to save our tigers and our family was going to end up *costing* us money. Cameras were pricey to fix. It was a disaster.

'It's still a good idea,' Joe said stoutly.

'But Dad won't let me use another camera!' I groaned. 'And we'd never get another shot like that one with Rabbit because it was one of those once-in-a-lifetime things that never happen twice, wasn't it? Why does this always happen to *me*?'

Tori came and sat next to me. She'd stopped laughing now. 'Joe's right,' she said. 'Animal modelling's an excellent idea.'

Mum had been looking confused through all of this. 'Animal *modelling*?'

'To make money so we don't have to send Chips and Gravy away,' I whispered.

Mum looked at me with her big chocolate-drop eyes.

Then she hugged me, even though I was still sopping wet and my clothes were going to leave big pond marks all over her shirt. I wasn't sure what she meant by the hug, but I was glad to get it all the same.

The kitchen door banged open. Dad stood there, his eyes blazing like comets. 'I just spoke to Mungo,' he said.

Mungo was an old mate of Dad's who worked in advertising. He had hairy toes and wore T-shirts with these names of old dinosaur rock bands on them like Pink Void.

'He told me last week about a pitch he's doing, for a catfood called Wow Miaow,' Dad said breathlessly to Mum. 'He thinks he can use the tigers instead of the cats he'd originally planned.'

'What have Chips and Gravy got to do with cats and football?' I asked in bewilderment. 'I mean, they're cats obviously. But—'

Dad gave this joyous laugh. He bent down and took my damp cheeks in his hands and kissed the bridge of my nose. 'An *advertising* pitch,' he said. 'It's what you put together to persuade a business that you've got the perfect way of selling their product. Mungo was telling me about his cats idea just the other day. Watching you filming the tigers made me think, Taya. What if Mungo suggested using *them* in his ad instead of cats?'

'But that man—' Mum began.

'He still won't know where the cubs are,' Dad said soothingly. 'And anyway, why would he know they were the cubs he stole? The last time he saw them, they were tiny. He doesn't know their new names. He doesn't know anything about us.'

'Is it safe for animals to work on film?' Mum said, still looking worried.

'The checks these production companies have in place when they use animals in films and adverts make sure the animals aren't harmed in any way,' Dad explained. 'They have welfare officers and vets coming out of their ears on set. Animals aren't permitted to work if they are injured or stressed or unwell. No harm can come to them. None at all.'

There was a light shining out of Dad, like he was some kind of weird human lampshade.

'I emailed Mungo some shots of the cubs I took last week. He's going to rewrite his pitch to include them,' he went on, wrapping his arms round Mum and kissing her neck. 'He was really excited. It wouldn't take much work to change what he'd already got, he said. He's showing it to the client tomorrow afternoon.

Now we just have to wait and see if Wow Miaow likes the idea. And if they do, then they'll pay to use Chips and Gravy.'

'How much?' said Tori, cutting to the important stuff as usual.

'More than I ever got photographing their cousins in Bengal,' said Dad.

'Nice one,' said Joe.

Talk about an understatement. Chips and Gravy and Rabbit all bounded in to the kitchen as everyone cheered and whooped and high-fived and low-fived and practically started disco-dancing on the table. The cubs stopped in shock and bounded straight out again. Rabbit barked happily and did a celebration bum skid across the kitchen floor.

Oh my wombats. Don't faint, but I'd just had my first good idea.

Floating is the best feeling. I mean, not *really* floating, obviously, but feeling like you are. One minute I was wishing I'd stayed at the bottom of the garden pond. And the next minute a fabulous future was flashing at my family like a bright and beautiful star. The cubs and all Mum's other animals safe and well and with us, where they belonged. Mum and Dad at home, running a business where everyone paid mega-bucks to film our gorgeous animals for films and ads and music videos. Tori and I might even get to be on TV ourselves. All of a sudden we were going to be insanely popular and famous, and Terry Tanner would slink off into the shadows. You couldn't get much more perfect than that. My plans for friendship with Cazza Turnbull suddenly moved up the queue. I'd tackle it tomorrow without fail.

'None of this is definite,' Dad warned once we'd all calmed down and the tigers had cautiously come back into the kitchen to sit in Rabbit's basket.

'We have to clear the idea with Wild World before we go any further,' Mum said. Her eyes were blazing with positive fire again. It was the first time I'd seen her look happy for weeks. 'And then if they agree that the cubs will be happy on a film set, we must have some kind of arrangement about the fee. The cubs aren't ours, remember.'

'Wild World will love it!' I said enthusiastically. 'They don't want to take the cubs away from you because they know you're the best person to look after them, Mum. Not that man. If there's any way of letting you keep them, they'll jump on it!'

'And even if Wild World agree, Wow Miaow has to

like the idea of using them to advertise their cat food,' Dad added. 'There are no certainties in advertising. Don't go around boasting about this to your friends, or you could end up looking very stupid.'

I wasn't listening. I was chatting about my famous life and my tigers with Cazza in the canteen, with everyone looking at me in envy. I was in Hollywood, posing by a piano-shaped swimming pool with Chips and Gravy on a matching pair of diamanté leads. It would be just like that bit in *Catwalk Talk* when the presenter Sylvie Dickens goes to these famous models' houses and goes 'Ooh!' over their wardrobes and then films them frying eggs in high heels and stroking their little white dogs.

'Don't worry, Dad,' said Tori. 'I won't say anything.'

'Me neither,' Joe promised.

'Hmm,' I said vaguely. What did it cost to fly to Hollywood?

Dad suggested ordering Chinese to celebrate the exciting news that Chips and Gravy were about to get famous. After Mum had insisted on getting dishes with the lowest sugar content for Dad, we sat around the table with the range ribbeting in the background and candlelight flickering on the walls. Joe ate a bit of every single thing that we ordered. I don't know where he put it because he's so skinny. Maybe inside his frankly enormous feet.

'Earth to Taya.'

I blinked. Was Tori talking to me?

'Our bus is here,' Tori said very slowly and very loudly. 'You have to climb up this step and then that one and show your pass and find somewhere to sit down. Can you remember this long and complicated list of instructions?'

'You promised you'd stop being sarcastic,' I said.

'I said I'd *try* not to be sarcastic,' Tori corrected. 'Right now that's too difficult.'

I pushed Joe up the steps in front of me, waved my pass and did this skipping thing down the aisle to our usual seat.

'You did listen when Dad reminded us how none of this is real yet, didn't you?' Tori checked as I sat down.

'Course I did,' I said. Should I mention our famous future to Cazza as soon as I saw her? I wondered. Might as well strike while the iron was hot. I was going to get tickets to film premieres and have movie stars to my birthday parties and who didn't want to be friends with someone like that?

'MO-RON!' chanted the Year Tens as they lumbered

on three stops later. Dwight Dingle put his head right up close to Joe and pulled a face. Joe flinched. 'MO-RON, MO-RON!'

'You'd think it would get stale, wouldn't you?' said Tori as the pack thundered on and swung up the steps to the top deck.

'Dwight Dingle's breath?' said Joe in a quiet voice in case the dinosaurs could hear him. 'It already did.'

My heart was somewhere in my throat as I watched the bus doors. The thought of telling Cazza our news – casually, of course – was making me feel ill with excitement. She'd be *amazed*. She'd be *speechless*. And at the first opportunity I'd spin out our story of fame and success and adverts.

Cazza hopped on board at the next stop with Cash 'n' Carrie. She didn't look at us, but as she went past she hissed like a snake. Although I wanted to be brave and follow her down the bus, I couldn't quite make my legs work. It could wait, I decided. I would enjoy the anticipation a bit more first.

Halfway through morning break, I made the mistake of entering the toilets.

'Hello, Weirdo.'

Cazza was beside the hand dryers.

Stay calm, Taya, I told myself. You're about to strike social gold.

I opened my mouth for the grand revelation.

'Tell your sister that she'd better watch out,' Cazza said. 'No one disses me in front of my mates and gets away with it. All right?'

Uh-oh. Cazza had obviously thought about things over half-term and decided that simply calling us weirdos every now and again wasn't having enough effect. Abandoning my immediate plans of friendship and fulfilment, I dashed into a cubicle and locked the door with trembling fingers. I sat down and tried to keep my head. Then I pulled the chain and walked out as steadily as I could. Cazza sniffed the air around me.

'Is that tiger poo on your shoes or did you just drop one?' she said softly.

'Our tigers are going on TV, actually,' I said, concentrating on washing my hands. 'And so are we.'

This wasn't strictly true, I know. But my life was at stake.

'So . . .' I continued, swallowing, 'don't be mean because soon we're going to know some really important and famous people. All right?'

It didn't sound as good as it had in my head.

'In your sad little safari park dreams,' Cazza snorted after a moment.

I dried my hands, pushed open the door and joined the stream of people in the corridor, all pushing and shoving and fighting their way to their classrooms as usual. I could hear Cazza's feet behind me. Bounce. Bounce. Bounce. Perhaps this was how it felt when you were in a cowboy film and this cowboy with a black shirt and black hat is following you into the saloon where you just know he's going to pick up a chair and crack you over the head with it. Bounce. Bounce. Bounce. She was catching up.

'I was on TV once,' Cazza said. Her black eyes slanted sideways at me across the corridor through her jet-black fringe. 'Reconstruction.'

Tori and Joe were a few metres ahead by our classroom door. They both frowned at the sight of me and Cazza side by side.

'See you then,' I said casually.

'Whatever,' said Cazza.

Which I took as a positive sign.

# 12

## Chocolate Sprinkles

'I can't believe you told Cazza the tigers would be on TV!' Tori fumed as I finally caught up with her at our gate that afternoon.

Tori had been steaming mad at me all day. We'd walked all the way back from the bus stop with her about ten metres in front of me like she was trying to escape. It was like the old days, when we pretended not to know each other, although because our faces were more or less exactly the same this had always been pretty hard to achieve.

'Don't be like this, Tor,' I panted. I was holding my side but trying not to show it. 'If I hadn't said anything she would have beaten me up. I haven't seen you looking too concerned about *that*.'

Tori whipped out her key with thunder still all over her face. 'We don't *know* if the tigers have got the job!' she said. 'Plus we don't know if Wild World has even agreed to let the tigers work. PLUS there's all these rules and regulations about using animals on TV and film that may be too difficult or too expensive. You never *think*, Taya! What if you've gone and made everything worse? If Wow Miaow don't want Chips and Gravy, we've lost them for ever and Terry Tanner might get his hands on them again. And we'll have to go back to Forrests with no tigers and none of this stupid fame that for some reason matters so much to you and . . . and . . .'

I was still on a bit of a cloud. Cazza had said 'All right?' to me *twice* in the corridor today. Social success was at my fingertips.

'Don't be so negative,' I said, interrupting Tori's breathless rant. 'Mungo said the tigers were exactly what he needed for his pitch. Wow Miaow would have to be idiots not to take them.'

We stepped through the front door. Mum was crying on the stairs with Gravy on her lap. I felt like the ceiling had just crashed down on my head. I swear, I heard the boom and saw the dust and everything. I even looked up to check. I didn't need to ask. I knew, just by looking at Mum's tragic crumpled face, that Wow Miaow had been idiots and turned the tigers down.

Tori and I sat in a dark patch on the stairs and stared at the chink of light and listened to the sounds that were seeping out from under the closed kitchen door. It was ten o'clock and we were supposed to have been in bed ages ago. Mum and Dad were talking.

'They're coming to collect the cubs tomorrow.'

'My agent is trying, but there is nothing for me. They say I'm too old! And I look at these young sticks they use today and I think OK, if you want to photograph a stick you can photograph a stick and sell your clothes and face creams and maybe sticks will buy your products but you will not sell a thing to women who are also *too old*.'

'Mum sounds furious,' Tori said.

'It must be awful to be told you're too old to do stuff,' I muttered. 'Anyway, her agent must be totally blind because Mum can SO keep modelling.'

Dad was still talking.

'I have a few small jobs lined up that will tide us over, love.'

'I wish . . .'

'Someone will hire you, Neet . . .'

'They're kissing,' I said gloomily as silence descended. 'Our life has turned into one of those tragic movies.'

I couldn't listen any more. I turned round like a zombie and shuffled up our spiral stairs with my head bowed, leaving Tori still sitting there. Chips was on Tori's bed and Gravy was lying like a large teddy bear on the rag rug in the middle of our room. The cubs knew it was their last night – I was sure of it.

After stroking and kissing them both and breathing in their warm fur I climbed slowly into bed and buried my head under my pillow. When Tori came up ten minutes later, I put my head out.

'You were right,' I whispered miserably. 'I've made everything worse.'

Tori lay on top of her bed and rested her cheek against Chips's back. 'Nothing is worse than this,' she said.

Downstairs, the phone rang a couple of times and then stopped. The house gave one of its weird creaks.

'Even the house is saying goodbye,' I sobbed.

'It's a house, Taya,' said Tori. 'It can't talk.'

I woke up groggily to find Gravy's nose pressed right up close to me. The moonlight that always got through our curtains on bright nights was reflecting off his eyes.

'You wanna go out?' I yawned. Finding my slippers I stumbled over and opened our bedroom door to go down. Chips came too. The cubs' huge paws lolloped down the spiral stairs and down again to the kitchen. Rabbit thumped her tail at us and got out of her basket. As I opened the back door, a gust of freezing night air rushed in and made the tiny hairs on my arms and legs stand up.

The moonlight was bright enough for me to see Rabbit and the tigers padding around the lawn, finding places to dig and do their stuff. Tigers are nocturnal, so they love the smells and sounds of night time. I rested against the doorframe and pulled my dressing gown tightly round me, watching and waiting. When they came back in again, the cubs got into Rabbit's basket. Rabbit headed for the rug Mum had put down beside the range. It looked pretty comfortable. So I lay down on it with my head close to Rabbit's back and watched the tigers settling down and then I closed my eyes too.

When I woke up in the morning, my neck was hurting. The tigers were lying on my legs, which had gone dead.

Mum was staring down at me, her bangled hands resting on her hips. 'Dad said you were here,' she said. 'I thought he was joking. You slept the night on Rabbit's rug?'

I sat up as best I could with dead legs. The tigers *vuvuv*ed at me, got up and had a little sniff around the kitchen, their tails brushing lightly against the corners of the kitchen cabinets as they marked our home as their home. Everything ached, especially my heart. And then I wanted to curl up and go back to sleep right then and there because I'd remembered something else about this awful day. Not only were the tigers leaving, but I had to face Cazza and everything was going to come out that the tigers weren't going on TV and I was basically a sad and tragic liar.

'I feel sick,' I whispered.

'You'll feel better after breakfast,' Mum said.

The thought of food made me want to puke. But Mum took me by the shoulders and sat me down at the table. There was a lovely spread all set out: cereal, butter, jam, a bowl of oranges, nice coffee in a pot. Even chocolate sprinkles, which we were normally only allowed to put on our toast on special days.

Tori came yawning into the kitchen. She shuffled to her place at the table and silently helped herself to cereal. She didn't look at me or Mum or even Rabbit, though I saw her eyes rest on the cubs for a millisecond.

'Your dad had a phone call late last night,' said Mum. She put some toast in the toaster and pressed it down.

'More bad news, I suppose,' I said. I poked the jam with my knife and wondered if toast would turn to dust in my mouth. 'Where is Dad, anyway?'

'Gone to London,' said Mum. 'A very important meeting with the people who do Double-Take.'

I rubbed a bit of sleep out of my eyes and hoped Mum would start making sense some time soon.

'What's Double-Take?' asked Tori.

'Shampoo,' I said. It was a really well-known make, and the kind of thing Tori just didn't know about. I had no idea what it had to do with Dad. It's not like he was big on hair products either.

'Is it a job then?' Tori asked with a frown.

'A job for the tigers!' Mum said joyfully. 'Someone else in Mungo's company showed your dad's pictures to the people at Double-Take. They want to use the cubs for their new TV advertisement. The paperwork is fine. The vets say it is fine. We can keep our animals, and Wild World will use their share of the money to invest in tiger research and a new tiger protection project in India. Terry Tanner can pay his lawyers as much as he likes, but Wild World will fight him all the way.'

Tori choked on her cereal. I turned white.

'A script is coming to us next week,' Mum said, her voice bubbling. 'It's true. Every word. The cubs are staying. We have won, *queridas*. We have won!'

# 13

## Paws, Claws and Applause

'Taya?'

I started back guiltily from Dad's closed study door.

'Stop standing outside my door.'

He couldn't know for *sure* I was outside his door. It wasn't like I was making any noise. Not like Amy Grittens in our class at Castle Hill, whose nose was permanently blocked so she sounded like Darth Vader with a cold.

'What?' I said, cupping my hand round my mouth so it sounded like I was really far away. 'I'm in the kitchen, Dad – I can't hear you!'

'I said, STOP STANDING OUTSIDE MY DOOR.'

'I'm not outside your door,' I said, still using the cupped-hand thing.

The door opened. Dad regarded me.

'Ah,' I said a bit feebly.

'As I've told you already three times today, I haven't read the Double-Take script yet,' said Dad. 'And if you keep breathing through the keyhole like a curious rhinoceros I'm not going to get round to it before next Tuesday.'

I gazed at the paper in his hand. 'Is that it?' I asked, starting forward to get a better look. 'Is there a part in it for me and Tori?'

'No.' Dad lifted the paper out of my eyeline. 'Please, Taya, go and help your mum and your sister. I'll be out as soon as I'm ready.'

It was worth one last shot.

'Are you sure I can't help *you*, Dad?' I said hopefully. 'I could read it through for you. Act it, maybe. To give you the proper feel.'

'There aren't any words, Taya,' Dad pointed out. 'It's a script for tigers.'

Faced with the choice between seeing my first ever real script and helping Mum and Tori do the washing up or the weeding or whatever, I got resourceful.

'I could pretend to be Chips,' I said. 'I'm good at tigers.'

Dad raised his voice. 'Neet? Tor? Can one of you

remove Taya before she drives me completely round the bend?'

Tori appeared from the garden. 'Come on, Kristen Stewart,' she said. 'No Oscar for you this year.'

If I wasn't going to get a chance to do any acting, I was determined to have a say in *something*. 'Have you thought of a name yet, Dad?' I called over my shoulder as Tori dragged me off.

'A name for what?' said Dad.

'For our new film business!'

'It's hardly a business yet, Taya,' said Dad, scratching his beard.

'But it could be,' I insisted. Was I the only one around here who was taking this seriously? 'We need a BRAND. We need T-shirts with a logo on and a website. I've got loads of names. Any time you want to hear them, you know where I am. How about Paws, Claws and Applause? I was pleased with that one though it's kind of long. Or—'

Dad had already shut his door.

'I'm only trying to help,' I moaned at Tori.

'No you aren't,' said Tori with her usual insight as she towed me outside. 'You're trying to skive weekend chores.'

'As if!' I said, doing my best to sound outraged. 'Our

new film business is work too, you know.'

Chips and Gravy had already bagged the sunniest spot in the garden and were grooming each other. Rabbit panted happily beside them, her eyes all squinty in the brightness. I paused for a moment and admired the way the sunlight caught the tigers' fur. They were going to be the most famous cats in England by the time we'd finished with them. We'd soon be fighting off invitations to sleepovers all over Fernleigh.

I hadn't renewed my attempts at friendship with Cazza over the past ten days. I'd just let things move at a gentle pace. She wasn't exactly lending me her rubber, but by the end of the week she'd got into this encouraging habit of nodding at me during registration. Definitely progress.

Mum was busy by the outside cages. She was wearing a really disgusting hat that looked like a brown felt flowerpot. I'm sorry, but it totally offended my fashion radar. What was she *thinking*?

'What IS on your head, Mum?'

'A hat is a hat, Taya,' Mum said, narrowing her almond-shaped eyes at me.

'Not when it looks like a wholemeal loaf!'

Mum brandished her pliers. 'Enough cheeky

remarks! Fetch some wire from the garage. Chips and Gravy will be moving into these cages very soon and we must make it safe.'

Heaving heavy wire mesh around wasn't exactly how I'd pictured spending my morning. I sighed, and followed Tori round to the garage.

'You shouldn't wind Mum up about the way she looks,' Tori warned me. 'She's very sensitive about it at the moment.'

I felt a bit guilty. It was easy to forget that in all this excitement, Mum was still dealing with the disappointment of being told she was too ancient to model any more. But the guilty feeling only lasted half a second before I was back on the hat.

'I thought Chips had done something nasty on her head,' I said.

This made Tori crack up. I don't make my sister laugh very often so I make the most of it. It makes me feel like the clever one for once.

'Funny now, is it?' I said, grinning.

'Mum can't see us here,' Tori spluttered. 'Kick me if I'm still laughing when we get back to the cages.'

I was about to heave the roll of mesh up with Tor when Joe appeared. His jeans weren't quite as short as his school trousers, but they still didn't reach his ankles.

I wondered if his dad ever put down his accountant's calculator and thought about taking Joe shopping. Judging from the trouser thing, probably not.

'What are you doing?' he asked.

I had a smart idea. 'Just something for the tigers,' I said carelessly.

Joe's eyes brightened. Anything to do with the animals and Joe would wade through man-eating mud. Or carry a ton of steel mesh. Which was, of course, the plan.

'What?' he said eagerly. 'Can I help?'

'It's quite important,' I said, sounding doubtful.

'I'm responsible,' Joe insisted. 'Let me do it. What is it?'

I heaved a sigh like I really didn't want him to. 'Well . . . It's this mesh for their cage,' I said at last. 'It's really important that we don't drop it because it has to be completely perfect for Mum to fix the tigers' cages. Otherwise the inspectors come and take away our licence to keep dangerous wild animals and then it's no more tigers or cheetahs or lions or *anything*.'

Somehow Joe missed Tori's snort. 'I'll take it,' he said immediately. 'You can trust me.'

I let Joe take my end of the mesh.

'Sucker,' said Tori under her breath from the front of

the mesh. I could tell she wished she'd thought of it herself.

'So when's the shoot?' Joe asked as he staggered after Tori round the side of the house.

I strolled along beside him, my hands in my pockets. 'Don't know yet. Dad's reading the script.'

'That's so cool,' Joe gasped.

Turning left past the end of the house was interesting. Joe's end of the mesh bashed against the side of the garage and he almost lost his grip. After staggering around like a comedy drunk person, he regained his balance.

'Is it OK?' he squeaked in horror. 'Have I dented it? Can your mum still fix the tigers' cages? Will the inspectors freak out?'

I soothed him with a pat. 'It's fine,' I said.

'So, what names have you thought of?' Joe said as we started walking again. 'For the film business?'

'Loads!' I said, delighted to be asked.

'I hope you've got a few that are better than Paws, Claws and Applause,' said my sister, bursting my happy balloon.

'What's wrong with Paws, Claws and Applause?' I demanded, stung. 'It rhymes and has a great rhythm.'

'I like it,' said Joe loyally.

'It's terrible,' Tori said.

'Well, if you're such a know-it-all, let's hear your ideas,' I challenged.

'We should keep it simple,' said Tori. 'Like The Animal Agency. Or Acting Animals.'

I gave a loud snore. 'Oh, sorry, fell asleep there for a minute. Is that seriously the best you can do? There's *loads* of great names we could use. Creatures on Camera. Fur on Film. Oscars and Whiskers— what?'

My sister was still laughing about Oscars and Whiskers when we got back to the cages, so I took great pleasure in kicking her, even though she wasn't laughing about Mum's hat.

It took a second to sink in that Chips and Gravy were in the middle of a MASSIVE fight.

# 14

# Hair is Never More Interesting than Tigers

When tigers fight, they make the scariest noise in the world. Both Chips and Gravy were crouched down close to the grass, their ears flat to their golden heads, making these awful deflating bagpipe noises that said, 'I am going to crunch your skull like a bag of Quavers when I can get close enough.' Now and again, one flashed out a heavy paw, claws unsheathed and gleaming in the sun, and swiped at the other with deadly intent.

Mum approached with a large bucket of water and tossed the freezing contents over both cubs. They leaped into the air, spitting with shock and water, then slunk to opposite sides of the garden to ignore each other. Rabbit watched them anxiously, her tail going round in circles. Every now and again the odd growl still wafted on the wind, like they couldn't quite drop the argument. I know what that feels like. You know how it is when you want to have the last word, no matter how long it takes?

We've seen our animals get nasty before. It's just a sign that they're growing up, testing each other out and getting territorial. But Joe looked like he was about to go into shock.

'Are the cubs all right?' he asked urgently. 'What got them so angry?'

'Hormones,' said Mum. She put the bucket down. 'Two boys fighting. That's all.'

'They'll go to their new home soon,' I told Joe. 'When they get like this, you know they're almost ready to leave.'

'New homeS,' Mum corrected. 'Sandown Safari and Yellowberry Park.'

'You're splitting them up?' Tori said with a gasp.

This was news to me too.

'Boy tigers can never stay together,' Mum explained. 'They are solitary animals. Wild World can't take either of them, so they are going to Sandown and Yellowberry instead.'

'But they love each other!' I protested. 'You can't split them up!'

'Tigers are not sentimental,' said Mum. Her eyes looked a bit shimmery. 'They'll be pleased to say goodbye when the time comes.'

We watched as Chips stalked back up the garden and settled in the sunny patch again. After a minute, Gravy joined him. Chips gave his brother a little nose kiss like nothing had happened.

'There,' said Mum as Gravy rested his big head between his paws. 'Friends again.'

But not for long. We all knew that. Living with wild animals is fantastic, don't get me wrong. But mixed in with the fun and the cuddles and the excitement there's painful bits too.

Dad came out of the house, shading his eyes against the sun with his hand. I still hadn't really got used to having him around the house all the time. But this alert, upright, enthusiastic Dad was a big improvement on the miserable grey skinny Dad from two months ago. He'd got much better about taking his insulin the right way and balancing his blood sugar levels than he had at the beginning, so we'd only had to dash to hospital once in the last week to sort him out. Balance came with practice, Doctor Nose had promised us. A bit like tightrope-walking.

'Hello, Joe,' he said. He nodded at the mesh that Joe was just dumping on the grass. 'Did Taya con you into carrying that?'

'No,' said Joe.

'Yes,' said Tori.

'What's the script like then, Dad?' I asked quickly as Joe gave me an uncertain glance. 'Any good?'

'Great,' Dad said. 'Provided we can get the cubs to do what the director wants.'

'Do we have to train them?' Tori asked.

My heart melted as I thought about the cublings doing tricks on telly. Chips juggling balls around with his big furry paws! Gravy breakdancing! Actually, Gravy already did breakdancing each time he wriggled about on his back having a scratch.

When I came out of my haze, Dad was explaining the ad.

'. . . so the actress is walking along beside the Serpentine – the big lake in Hyde Park in London. And she's got the cubs on two leads, walking quietly.'

Tori shot a doubtful glance at the cubs. They gazed back, calm again after their fight and completely unconcerned. Mum gave a hollow laugh.

'Chips and Gravy never do *anything* quietly,' I said.

'In theory, they're quiet,' Dad amended. 'That's where the training will come in. So anyway. She's walking along, and her hair's all bouncy and shiny thanks to Double-Take.'

'Glowing with radiance,' I added, following the storyline closely.

Dad looked puzzled. 'What?'

'It means shiny in ad-speak,' I explained. 'Glowing with radiance.'

'Sounds a bit radioactive,' said Tori.

'Can I continue?' Dad enquired. 'She's walking along and all these people are looking at her. You think they're looking at the cubs. But then the cubs come off their leads –' he double-checked the script '– and everyone is still watching our shiny-haired lady. Ergo, Double-Take hair is more interesting than tigers.'

'Hair is never more interesting than tigers,' Tori said.

'If I saw a lady walking two tigers and they came off their leads?' said Joe. 'I wouldn't watch the lady.'

'I don't think they're aiming the ad at you, Joe,' I said.

Hair is important and everything and without it your head would get well cold and there's loads of fun stuff you can do with it, but I did actually think my sister and Joe were right. I mean, seriously? You'd check out a lady's hairstyle over a pair of adorable Bengal tiger cubs?

'Well, the people at Double-Take think it'll work,' said Dad cheerfully. 'And I'm not about to complain.'

Something clunked into place. *Actress*. So there *was* an actress after all!

'What actress are they going to use?' I asked eagerly, deciding not to give Dad a hard time about fibbing to me outside his study. 'Is it someone famous?'

'Whoever they are, they'll have fabulous hair,' said Dad.

He said *fabulous* in this hilarious voice that cracked me up. Mum gloomily tucked her own hair up under her flowerpot hat. Dad put his arm around her shoulder and rubbed gently at her neck.

'So they want us to train the cubs to walk quietly and come off their leads at the right moment?' Tori checked.

'That's right.' Dad glanced at the cubs, who were now both upside down and snoring with Rabbit curled up blissfully in between. 'And we're going to get through a *lot* of beef treats to achieve it. The shoot is in London next weekend.'

I squealed with excitement. London! Oxford Street!

Harrods! The London Eye! 'Can we come too?' I begged. 'Can we, Dad? Can we, can we, can we?'

'We couldn't do it without you,' Dad said. 'Who else would fetch us cups of tea for free?'

Before Tori and I could leap into a victory dance using Joe as a maypole, Mum interrupted. 'If you want to come,' she said, 'it will be like the time we first had the cubs. You must help us every day after school with their training. There will be no dates at your friends' houses. There will be no after-school clubs.'

'Fine by us,' said Tori, exchanging shining glances with me.

Joe was hopping from one giant trainer to the next like the grass was the range on full, his face glowing with hope.

'Joe?' I said generously. 'Would you like to come and help as well?'

'It means no chess club,' Tori said, like *that* was any great loss.

'I would *love* to,' Joe said in a fervent voice.

'I'm sorry, but we can't take you to London too, Joe,' said Mum, sounding regretful.

Joe took the disappointment on the chin. 'That's fine. I think my dad's at home next weekend anyway.'

'There will be a lot to do on Saturday morning,

girls,' Dad warned me and Tori as we grinned stupidly at each other. 'Washing and grooming and making sure the tigers are presentable. You'll have to help us with that as well.'

'No problem!'

'Great,' Dad said. 'We'll be up at five a.m.'

*Five a.m.?* I guess not everything about fame is glamorous.

Somehow, Tori and I got through the week without a detention even though we didn't listen to a THING any of the teachers said because we were so busy planning our trip to London. Even Cazza, an expert at messing about, got one for throwing Carrie's bag on the roof of the science block.

'It's a sign,' I said jubilantly as the Friday bell went and we joined the school corridor racetrack.

'It's a sign that we're invisible,' Tori said. 'That usually drives me mad. You know, when you put your hand up because you know the answer to the algebra problem on the whiteboard and the teacher calls someone else?'

I looked at my sister blankly. 'Not a feeling I know, Tor,' I said.

Tori was still expanding on her theory. 'Because we're

basically not much trouble and quite clever – well, I am anyway – the teachers *actually can't see us*. Which is very useful when you've got stuff on your mind and aren't concentrating. Cazza only has to breathe and Ms Hutson is on her back.'

I grasped the only bit of Tori's rant that I'd caught. 'What do you mean, *you're* clever?'

'Hiya, can I come back to yours?'

It was Joe, surfing out of the cloakroom with a bunch of other Year Seven boys, his coat hung on his head by the hood like he was a peg. He'd come back to ours every day that week to help with the training. Which, incidentally, wasn't going well.

'Course you can,' I said.

'Let's face it,' Tori added, 'Mum and Dad need all the help they can get.'

'MO-RON!' shouted Dwight Dingle, barging down the corridor with his arms out like an aeroplane. For once, he didn't have his mates with him. The kids nearby ducked. You learn from experience when Dwight Dingle is around. 'MO-RON! MO-RON!'

Tori grabbed Joe by one arm and I grabbed him by the other and we fled. We ran so fast we caught the early bus home.

* * *

Back at ours, we sat on the damp grass and ate crisps as we watched Mum and Dad doing the training, like we had every day that week. Every now and again they would yell for more meat, so we took turns fetching it from the back fridge. The only things that motivate boy tigers are food and lady tigers, apparently. As we didn't have a lady tiger available, our local butcher thought Christmas had come early.

Even with stacks of meat, tigers are not easy to train. In fact, you might have more luck training a brick. At least a brick stays where you put it and doesn't go off in search of food or to roll in a dead hedgehog it's found in the bushes.

'But why isn't he DOING it?' I said in exasperation after Chips had followed Mum for the millionth time instead of staying still, despite the fact that she'd let him off his special-release lead.

'It's because Mum's hands smell of meat,' Tori said.

'There's a disease like that,' said Joe. 'It's when your sweat smells of rancid chicken and no matter how many showers you have you still stink. I read it on the Internet.'

'This is totally gross,' I said, briefly diverted from the view of Mum yelling at Dad and stomping down the garden again with the empty lead swinging from her hand and Chips trotting next to her with his nose pressed into her palm.

On top of Chips not doing what he was told, the special-release leads were proving tricky. If you pressed them wrong, they didn't release at all. Plus Gravy was snoozing on top of the carrot patch and refusing even to let Mum put the lead on him in the first place, which wasn't improving Mum's temper.

Mum looked frozen to the bone. The November wind knifed us like a crazed chef with too many potatoes to peel.

'Why don't you move to a sunnier bit of the garden, Mum?' I suggested, shivering in my coat.

Mum wiped her forehead, pushing back her manky hat as she did. I shuddered to think of her face now smelling of beefy bits. 'Why?' she asked, sounding exhausted. 'You think it will help?'

'Probably not,' I said. 'But at least you'll be warmer.'

'Taya's right,' said Dad, wrestling Gravy off the carrots and coaxing the lead round his golden neck with yet *another* bit of meat. 'You are turning blue, love.'

Mum and Chips moved further up the garden as Dad hauled Gravy on to his gigantic paws and along to join his brother. They were now quite close to the pond, which twinkled and shimmered in the sunlight. It looked inviting even to me, and I'm not a water-obsessed tiger cub.

'I hope the cubs don't pull Mum into the pond,' Tori said, reading my mind as usual. 'It's hard enough controlling one of them past that water, let alone two.'

'Mum'll be fine,' I said, not feeling sure about this at all.

'It's good to practise by water,' said Joe. 'They'll have to walk past the Serpentine lake for the ad, won't they?'

I'd forgotten that. 'Good point, Joe,' I said. 'Have another crisp.'

Mum took hold of both leads and braced her feet in the grass as the cubs looked expectantly at Dad, Chief Bearer of Beefy Bits. Dad looked hard at the script and scribbled something in a fat red pen down the margin, then scratched his cheek with the wrong end of the pen and left this long red slash across his face like Chips had just clawed him. 'OK,' he said. 'You ready, Neet?'

Mum nodded and grabbed the tigers' leads more tightly, like a warrior queen seizing the reins to her chariot.

'Then ... action. Good ... Keep going ... still good ...'

Chips and Gravy both paused at the edge of the pond. Chips's eyes glinted. Mum's eyes widened.

'Neet, they're—'

'Mum!'

'CHIPS!!'

'Release the lead! Release the—'

There was a splosh as the cubs hit the water. Still wrestling with the release thingy on their leads, Mum went in next. We all rushed to help her out of the pond while Chips and Gravy happily flung themselves around like a couple of stripy seals. Then Chips leaped out of the pond again and shook himself, followed closely by his brother. Droplets of ice-cold water flew over everyone. By everyone, I mean mainly me.

'I guess the release things didn't work,' said Joe, staring at the leads still round the cubs' necks.

A withering look is difficult to pull off when your fringe is wet and pond water is dripping in your eyes. But I managed it.

'No kidding, Sh-Sh-Sherlock,' I said through my chattering teeth.

# 15

## The Most Famous Hair on TV

Five o'clock in the morning is not a good time. Everything's still dark when it's November, and completely freezing as well. We were all gathered in the animals' bathroom downstairs, trying not to feel weird about how the moon was shining through the window, and preparing the cubs for their big day.

'Shampoo,' Mum said, holding out her hand like she was a surgeon conducting a complex heart bypass operation.

Tori gave her the bottle of special animal shampoo. Chips squirmed blissfully in the warm water, turning on his back so Mum could shampoo his tummy. He flicked his tail playfully.

'Urgh!' I squealed, getting my second drenching in

two days. I was having trouble keeping hold of Gravy, who was keen to join his brother in the tub. 'Chips, keep your tail still, will you?'

While Dad towelled Chips down, Gravy leaped into the water for his turn. Most of the water leaped out and soaked Rabbit, who reversed out of the bathroom with a yelp.

'Mop!' shouted Mum.

No sooner had Tori mopped the floor than it got wet again. The tigers were going mental. It was dark, and they were having baths. Talk about tiger paradise. Chips escaped Dad's towel and shook the rest of the bathwater all over the kitchen, while Gravy avoided the towel completely and rolled all over the bathroom mat instead. We all got the giggles really badly. All the excitement meant Rabbit lost it, chasing her tail in a creaky kind of way and bumskidding down the hall.

At last, we loaded the clean and sparkly cubs into their cages in the back of our big black van.

'Have we got the leads?' Dad said, getting into the driving seat.

'Check,' said Tori, holding the leads up. We had three sets in case two broke.

'Meat?'

'Check,' I said, looking at the massive icebox full of

beef bits at my feet with a slight shudder.

'Water? Tiger poo bags?' Dad went on. 'Children?'

'Check,' me and Tori chorused.

'Medicine, Dad?' said Tori.

Dad brandished his insulin pen from out of his top pocket. 'Wife?' he said finally.

Silence.

'Wife?' Dad bellowed.

Mum came hurrying out of the house, her horrible hat pulled even further down her head than normal to keep out the cold. 'I am here,' she panted. 'I was just feeding Fernando and Sufi. Oh, and we must drop Rabbit at the Mortons'!'

She dashed back inside, pulled Rabbit out on her lead and pushed her up into the van, where her big golden bottom took up most of Mum's seat and her tail swished over Dad's hand as he changed gear. We set off down the drive, Dad's fingers drumming on the steering wheel. Even though we still had plenty of time, he was as jumpy as a flea. In the back Chips and Gravy were wide awake and more than a little bit interested in what was going on.

We trundled through the gate, the van's headlights catching a little fox snooping around the apple trees. Automatically I checked for strange cars in case Terry

Tanner had found us, but it was a bit tricky in the dark.

At the Mortons' place, Joe was already waiting, looking totally blissed out as Mum climbed out and handed Rabbit over. His dad had agreed that they would look after Rabbit while we were in London. Which basically meant Joe could pretend to be a pet owner for the day. We suspected Rabbit was about to get the walk of her life.

In the night I'd thought of a new name for our business, and was well excited about it. Having a captive audience in the van for an hour wasn't an opportunity to be wasted.

'I've got a new name,' I began as we hit the motorway.

'But Taya's a lovely name,' said Dad. 'Why have you changed it?'

'Not *my* name, Dad,' I said. 'The business. We should call it Tall Tails!'

There was silence.

'Why is it tall?' Mum said eventually.

'It's an expression meaning stories,' I explained. 'And you spell Tails like tails, not tales,' I added, just to be clear.

'I don't understand,' said Mum with a frown.

'Strike one,' said Tori. 'Ow!'

We bickered the rest of the way up to London, and only shut up when finally Dad cracked at the Hyde Park gates and told us he wouldn't bring us next time.

Even though it was still dark in the park, there were loads of people wrapped up in coats and hats and those bright-yellow jackets that give you a headache if you look at them for too long. Most of them were waving clipboards, and everyone looked busy. Huge lights were everywhere, so bright they made me squint nearly as much as the jackets did. My quarrel with Tori faded from my mind. I felt shivery with excitement. We were on a *real live film set*!

As Tori and I helped Mum unlock the back of the van, a harassed-looking lady with bright blonde spiky hair rushed up to us. 'Andy Wild?' she said, looking at Dad. 'The tiger guy?'

'The Tiger Guy!' I gasped, spinning round to Tori.

Tori knew I was still going on about a name for the business. 'We can't change the name from animal to animal,' she pointed out. 'The Animal Guy would work, maybe?'

'I am not a guy,' Mum pointed out in a frosty voice.

Tori and I exchanged silent glances. It was very easy to rile Mum at the moment. Her fashion offences were getting more serious too. Today she was wearing baggy brown trousers and boots covered in mud.

While Dad talked to the spiky-haired lady – who turned out to be the director – we got the cubs out of their cages. They both looked beautiful. Their fur was all fluffy and clean, their ears alert and swivelling on their stripy heads like tiny satellite dishes and their eyes bright with excitement. After Gravy had sniffed Mum's hat in case it was a dead animal, they gazed around the bustling film set expectantly. Lots of people stopped hurrying and started pointing and smiling. I pulled myself up and sucked in my tummy like the models always do on *Catwalk Talk* even though you probably couldn't tell through my mega-thick puffer jacket.

'They aren't looking at you, Taya,' Tori said.

'Goodness, aren't they *gorgeous*!' said the director, whose name was Paula. The worry lines on her face fell away as she gazed rapturously at the cublings. 'I've *never* seen tiger cubs up so *close*. Their markings are *exquisite*!'

I decided I liked Paula. Mum did too. With her voice sounding softer than it had in ages, Mum was soon telling the director the story of Terry Tanner.

'What a *scandal*!' Paula gasped every now and again. 'Simply *ghastly*!'

Listening to Paula was like waiting for a ball to bounce. She kept putting all this weight on particular words. Talk, talk, *bounce* a word; talk, talk, *bounce* a word. Soon I was listening for the *bounce* and not hearing the words at all. I started to feel like a hypnotized snake in a basket.

The most delicious smell of frying bacon came wafting towards us from a shiny metal bus with a special hatch in the side, breaking the spell.

'Get us all a bacon sarnie from the canteen, will you girls?' said Dad. 'No cash needed. Just tell them you're with the cubs.'

He glanced sideways at Mum. His diabetes meant he wasn't supposed to have a sandwich without an injection – and a fatty sarnie was especially unhealthy. But Mum either wasn't listening or decided that one sarnie wouldn't do any harm, because she just nodded.

We handed over the cubs' leads and dashed over to join the line at the canteen bus. I squinted down the line, looking hopefully for famous faces. All I saw were stubbly chins and smudged mascara and quite a lot of yawning. It struck me that everyone looked more or less the same as our teachers on a bad morning.

We'd been waiting for a few minutes, listening to the crew chatting about mystifying things like rushes and gaffers, when a lady with long red hair marched past us all waving a bacon sandwich at the catering manager.

'This sandwich is a disgrace! Have you any idea how bad this kind of thing is for a model's skin?'

The catering manager leaned out of the hatch on a pair of brawny black arms. 'Bacon sarnies are bacon sarnies, love,' he said. 'Not healthfood.'

'What a silly woman,' said Tori in disgust as the lady shouted some more about reporting the catering van's excessive use of transfats to Health and Safety.

I wasn't listening. I was staring mesmerized at the lady's hair. It was probably the most famous hair on TV. I'd just seen it flicking about on telly the night before.

'That's . . .' I stuttered. 'Th . . . th . . . that's . . .'

'A very stupid woman, yes,' Tori said. 'I mean, honestly! No one *made* her order that bacon sandwich.'

I managed at last to get my words out. 'Tor,' I croaked. 'It's *Sylvie Dickens*!'

# 16

## I Am So TOTALLY Your Biggest Fan

Tori said nothing. This was disappointing. When you get a bombshell like the fact that Sylvie Dickens is on the same film set as you, it's fair to expect at least a bang of some kind.

'Oh my wombats,' I said, suddenly understanding as we headed back to the van with our bacon sandwiches. 'You don't know who Sylvie Dickens is, do you?'

'Nope,' Tori said.

Only my sister wouldn't know who Sylvie Dickens was. She can name most of the stars in our galaxy, but our country's most famous model presenter? Uh – no.

'Sylvie Dickens is the presenter of *Catwalk Talk*,' I said carefully. 'She has been at the top of the modelling industry for nearly ten years and is married to some mega-bucks millionaire. She's on the front of *heat* and *Grazia* practically every single week. Sound familiar yet?'

I glanced back over my shoulder to see Sylvie Dickens hurling her bacon sandwich towards the shore of the Serpentine, where a couple of ducks looked at it before a small black dog belonging to one of the cameramen wolfed it down with a guilty look on its face.

'That's exactly the look she does in that ad campaign for animal print handbags that's all over the billboards in Fernleigh, the one where she snarls straight at the camera!' I gasped.

'Let go of my arm,' Tori growled. 'You're compromising my circulation.'

A fresh wave of excitement hit me. 'She must be *the actress*! Mum and Dad are here to work with *Sylvie Dickens*!'

'And we're here to work with the cubs,' said Tori. 'So that makes us just as important as her.'

This was an interesting point that almost made me choke on my sarnie. If we were just as important as Sylvie, then Sylvie wouldn't mind me popping over to her trailer, would she? You know, just to say hello.

We reached Mum and Dad and handed over the sarnies.

'I, er, think I fancy another one,' I said, giving Chips's head a quick rub and backing away. 'I'll be back in a minute.'

Leaving Tori brushing Gravy's tail, I half ran, half walked through the brightening morning to the shiny silver trailer Sylvie had stormed off to. Feeling giddy with terror and excitement, I watched with horrible amazement as my hand lifted up *of its own accord* and knocked on the trailer door.

'—not enough coverage. I can't forge a decent career if the press start to forget who I am. Sort it out, or I'll be looking for another agent. Clear?'

Sylvie Dickens snapped her bright-pink phone shut and looked at me. 'Yes?'

A thousand thoughts rushed into my head about the coolest way to start a conversation with the most stylish woman on TV. Then they rushed out again.

'Oh my wombats I am so TOTALLY your biggest fan!' I said.

Sylvie smiled. She had incredible teeth.

'I just wanted to say hello,' I stuttered. 'I'm here with the tiger cubs!'

'Cute,' she said.

'They are,' I agreed happily. I was in a total daze. Me and Sylvie were *chatting*. 'You have to come and meet them! They're looking totally adorable today because we washed them and dried them but not with Double-Take, ha ha! We've been training them all week to walk on their leads like little stripy lambs. I know they'll be really good with you!'

'Sure they will, sweetie,' said Sylvie. 'I'm needed for make-up and hair now. I'll see them later.'

She started closing the trailer door.

'Can I help?' I asked eagerly, catching the edge of the door. 'I'm great with make-up. And hair too! Or your script? If you need any help with that—'

'No thanks, honey,' said Sylvie. Her eyes were like sapphires.

'You don't know how cool this is!' I said, unable to help myself. 'Until two weeks ago we thought we were going to lose the cubs totally and then this ad came along!'

The trailer door started opening again.

'Reeeaaaally?' said Sylvie.

'It was awful,' I confided. 'Dad fell ill and we nearly had to return the cubs to the Wild World safari park who maybe were going to give the cubs back to Terry Tanner – this horrible man who took the cubs from

India in the first place but that's a different story – because Dad didn't have any work and Mum had to go and find a different job. But now everything's fine!'

'TAYA!'

I looked round to see Mum waving at me. And not in a friendly *how are you doing?* kind of way. More like *what are you doing and why aren't you doing it over here?*

'Got to go,' I said regretfully. 'I'll see you later, though! I'll give Chips and Gravy big kisses from you!'

I floated back to the van on a cloud.

'Been making friends with our star?' enquired Dad, rubbing Gravy between the ears.

'She's a diva,' said Tori.

I felt offended on Sylvie's behalf. 'She was perfectly lovely to me,' I said. 'Really sympathetic about the cubs and Terry Tanner and everything.'

'You don't go telling strangers about Terry Tanner, Taya,' Mum said in a sharp voice.

'I only told her what you told Paula,' I objected, feeling a bit annoyed at Mum's double standards. 'Anyway, we're keeping the cubs until they find a permanent home now we've got this new business, aren't we? Terry Tanner is history!'

'Rich men who don't get what they want first time will always try again,' Mum said.

I blinked. Terry Tanner *wasn't* history?

As I was processing Mum's little bombshell, a gentle-looking man with hair like a badger's approached and introduced himself as Kalim Ahmed, set vet.

'Do all films that use animals have a vet on site then?' I asked, trying to put the spectre of Terry Tanner out of my head as Kalim shook everyone's hands.

'Always for advertisements, sometimes for TV and films,' said Kalim. He had a gap between his two front teeth when he smiled. 'The directors can't use animals who show signs of stress or illness. It's my job to make sure the animals are healthy and happy.'

Gravy jumped on Chips's back and started chewing his brother's ears. Kalim looked at the cubs and grinned. 'They seem pretty healthy to me,' he said.

As Dad went through the paperwork with Kalim, another man walked slowly towards us, clutching yet another clipboard. He was very tall and thin, in a grey suit and long beige raincoat. Catching sight of him, Kalim sighed.

'Sylvester Spock,' he told Dad. 'Animal Welfare Officer. Not an easy customer.'

'What's the difference between him and you?' Tori asked as Sylvester Spock came closer. He had a strange, stiff way of walking.

'He's not a vet,' said Kalim.

'He looks like a stork,' Mum said.

Mum tends to say what she's thinking out loud, no matter how rude.

'Mum!' Tori hissed.

Mum shrugged. 'It's true. He walks like he has a stick up his—'

'Sylvester!' said Kalim loudly. 'Come and meet the Wilds and their tigers. Sylvester represents Animals UK, a welfare charity with particular interest in animals on film sets.'

Sylvester Spock even held his chin like a stork's beak. It stuck out and bobbed when he moved. He looked disapprovingly at the cubs. 'Are these the animal actors?' he said.

I didn't dare look at Tori. I knew I would explode with laughter. I couldn't help picturing a pair of long yellow stork legs inside his trousers.

'Yes, Mr Stork,' said Dad. 'I mean, Spock. Chips and Gravy.'

Tori made a grunting noise as a laugh escaped. I snorted too. We both stared frantically at the ground. The cubs stopped chewing each other and gazed at Mr Spock with curious golden eyes.

'Chips and Gravy,' Sylvester Spock repeated, flicking

his eyes at me and Tor. 'Not very dignified names, are they?'

'Funny names don't contravene any animal welfare act I know,' said Dad.

Sylvester Spock produced a pencil and started writing on his clipboard. 'Food and water?' he snapped out.

Mum pointed to the bowls of water we'd set aside for the cubs and the icebox full of meat.

Sylvester Spock narrowed his eyes at the cubs, taking in their well-brushed fur and clear eyes. 'General appearance?'

'They look like tigers to me, Mr Spock,' said Dad.

Kalim Ahmed hurriedly turned a laugh into a cough.

Looking displeased, Sylvester Spock tucked his pencil into his top pocket. 'I shall be watching you very closely,' he said. 'Animals UK actively campaigns against the use of animals on film, where creatures cannot exhibit their natural behaviour. If I find that you are in breach of any part of the 1925 Performing Animals Act or indeed the Dangerous Wild Animals Act of 1976, I will have no hesitation in filing a complaint and having you shut down!'

# 17

## Snail With a Limp

Sylvester Spock suddenly wasn't looking as funny as before.

'As if we'd harm Chips and Gravy!' I said, recovering from the shock as he stalked away. 'How dare he! All that stuff about exhibiting natural behaviour. Does he want them running around Hyde Park chasing deer and joggers?'

'He didn't even say hello to the cubs,' said Tori indignantly. 'What kind of Animal Welfare Officer isn't actually interested in animals?'

'Mr Spock is only doing his job,' said Dad in the kind of voice he uses when trying to convince himself that the sweetener in his coffee is just as nice as sugar.

'Ha!' said Mum, who had been unusually silent up till now. 'We will give Mr Stork natural behaviour. We will send the cubs to bite his skinny stork ankles! He knows nothing of their suffering as they are taken from their home by Mr Terry Tanner and his Big Enormous Cheque Book. He knows nothing of their need for security and love and beefsteak. He can go and nest in a chimney far away from here.'

'Ignore my wife,' Dad advised Kalim. 'She gets a little overprotective of the animals in her care.'

'I meet Sylvester Spock on set all the time,' Kalim said. 'He means what he says about shutting you down. Don't get on the wrong side of him.'

'I think we already did,' said Tori.

Sylvester Spock was deep in conversation with Paula, the director, by the water's edge. Judging from his jabbing fingers, he was giving her a hard time about the cruelty of putting tigers on telly.

'We'd better go and help,' Dad said. 'Good to meet you, Kalim. Girls, watch the cubs, will you?'

'Filming isn't nearly as much fun as I thought it would be,' I said gloomily, sitting in the open back of the van and stroking Chips's head as Kalim went to have a chat with some lighting guys and Mum and Dad headed down to join Sylvester Spock and the director. There was still no sign of Sylvie Dickens emerging from her trailer.

'I'm missing *Doctor Who Confidential* for this,' Tori said, tickling Gravy in a spot just under his chin that he loved.

The crew stood around looking even more bored than us as Sylvester Spock produced a large document and started flicking through it, pointing out sections to Paula, who looked like she was having a really bad day. Mum and Dad hovered helplessly. Kalim joined in, producing more paperwork. The catering van was doing a roaring trade in bacon sarnies. Time oozed by like a snail with a limp.

About a million years later, Sylvester Spock backed off and filming began.

'Wow!' I gasped as Sylvie Dickens came out of her trailer at last. She stood by the water's edge, wearing a fabulous red wool coat belted at the waist. Her hair glowed with so much radiance it was giving the weak November sun a complex. Hair and make-up assistants buzzed around, flicking a brush here and a powder puff there.

'*Lovely*, Sylvie!' called Paula, sounding relieved that everything was at last underway. 'Everyone set? We're running out of time *already*, guys – we *have* to get as much as we can before our licence expires at midday. *Action!*'

We watched as Sylvie swayed down the side of the Serpentine, the wind in her face so her hair blew the right way, a camera on a set of traintracks running along beside her.

'Why aren't they filming with the cubs yet?' I asked.

'I think they just want close-ups of Shirley first,' Tori told me.

'It's *Sylvie*, you geek. Ooh!' I gasped as Sylvie did the Ultimate Hair Toss. 'Did you see that? I bet they'll use a slow-mo shot. It was *fierce*.'

Pulling the scrunchie out of my hair, I practised tossing it around the way Sylvie was doing.

'You look like a pony with flies in its ears,' Tori said.

Mum brushed Gravy's fur for the hundredth time. The cubs were getting restless. Dad had already stopped Chips from chewing the tyres on the van. We would have to exercise them soon.

'Cut!' Paula shouted at last. '*Nice* start, everyone. Shall we try a *tiger* shot? Sylvie, how do you *feel* about that?'

Sylvie was gazing around. She appeared to be looking for someone. 'Whatever,' she said, her eyes on the horizon and her foot tapping impatiently.

Paula looked our way. 'Tigers?'

'This is us,' said Dad.

I flipped into panic mode. 'Where are the leads?' I squealed as I jumped up and ran to the front of the van, then back again. 'Did we forget the leads? What do we do? What now?'

Mum held the leads up. I sheepishly attached Gravy's while Tori did Chips's. The cubs' fluffy ears went on alert, and they walked as meek as pussycats down with us to where Sylvie was waiting, their tails sweeping along behind them like huge fluffy pipe cleaners.

The crew all came over and made a fuss, tickling Chips's ears and marvelling at how long Gravy's tail was. I beamed at Sylvie, who didn't beam back. She probably didn't want to crack her make-up.

'Good to meet you, Miss Dickens,' said Dad. 'Here are your co-stars, Chips and Gravy.'

There was an odd look in Sylvie's eyes as she gazed at the cubs. A mixture of greedy and frightened, if that makes sense. 'They're not as cute as I remember,' she said at last. 'Do they bite?'

'Only if you're the postman,' said Tori.

In the background, Sylvester Spock was hovering like a fart in assembly, still writing things on his clipboard. Mum nudged Tori, who shut up. I was thinking about what a strange thing Sylvie had just said. She'd never met the cubs before. What did she mean, not as cute as she remembered?

'They'll be fine,' Dad assured Sylvie. 'We've hand-reared them since they were newborns. Here are their leads. You see this button? When Paula calls "release", you press—'

'I'll work it out,' Sylvie said coolly. She peered off into the distance, looking for whatever she was looking for. 'It can't be that hard.'

'It's harder than it looks,' Dad said.

A look of deep irritation crossed Sylvie's face. 'I *said*, I'll work it out.'

'See?' said Tori under her breath as I blinked at Sylvie's tone of voice. 'Diva.'

'She's just a professional,' I said, a little uncertainly.

Sylvie took the leads. Chips and Gravy sat on the ground, their tails twitching just a tiny bit. Mum and Dad stepped back, exchanging glances.

'She really should practise with those leads,' Tori said.

I completely agreed. The thought of Sylvie Dickens – not to mention her very expensive and fabulous red coat – ending up in the lake because of the cubs made me feel a little ill.

'Just walk up and *down* a bit, Sylvie,' Paula encouraged. 'Get the *feel*. OK? Everyone OK?'

Sylvie's roving eyes finally settled on something that made her relax. She shot a dazzling smile at the cubs and did another fabulous hair toss as a photographer appeared, pushing through the crowd.

'Sylvie!' shouted the photographer. 'Give us a smile, Sylvie!'

'This is a closed set,' Paula said indignantly to the photographer, who was blasting off his camera like a laser gun as Sylvie smiled and laughed. 'Miss Dickens is not available for paparazzi shots just now.'

'Just a few shots won't hurt, Paula,' said Sylvie, batting her long black eyelashes at the photographer.

Another person appeared, holding a tiny digital recorder. Ignoring Paula's spluttering protests, he thrust it up to Sylvie's smiling, perfectly lipsticked mouth.

'Is it true you're starring in this campaign to save these adorable tiger cubs from being put down, Sylvie?'

I laughed. Where did journalists get such stupid questions?

'What funny stories you hear!' Sylvie tinkled, winking prettily at the cameras. 'It's not quite as bad as that!'

'But surely you can tell us the real story?' pressed the journalist as Paula squawked like a useless parrot in the background.

And then the weirdest thing happened. Sylvie Dickens stopped smiling. Tears shone in the corners of her heavily made-up eyes. Her whole face crumpled tragically. It reminded me of a play I saw once, when this woman collapsed artistically on the stage when this other woman pretended to shoot her.

'The real story?' she said. 'Oh yes. I can tell you the real story.'

The journalist looked well excited. He held his recorder thing even closer to Sylvie's trembling red lips as she hunkered down and gathered the cubs in to her.

'These were once my babies,' she said huskily. 'But they were taken from me. And I will give everything I have to get them back.'

# 18

## The Hoover of Forgetfulness

I was so shocked by Sylvie's wacko announcement that the smile fell off my own face faster than a bobsled down an icy track. Had we entered a parallel world? Was this a different kind of film set from the one I'd been expecting; a movie set with a crazy tiger storyline?

Totally unaware of the stir they were causing, Chips and Gravy let Sylvie fuss over them like a couple of teddy bears. Chips even started washing his ears, causing a volley of camera shots. I looked round helplessly at my family. Everyone looked like they'd just run off a cliff and were left pumping their legs in thin air.

'You know you said this Shirley—' Tori began.

'Sylvie,' I whispered, still in shock.

'—was married to some billionaire, Taya? Well, his name isn't – Terry Tanner, by any chance?'

'Of course not! It's . . .'

A magazine page shimmered in my memory. *Sylvie Dickens (32) throws lavish pink champagne party for husband Terry's fiftieth birthday.*

Oh. My. Wombats.

Dad covered his eyes. Mum made this awful growling noise, and swivelled very slowly on her heel to fix Sylvie Dickens with the full force of her laser-beam eyes. I was having a complete out-of-body experience. Could this really be true? Was Sylvie Dickens, *Catwalk Talk* presenter and my complete heroine, the dimwit wife of my nightmares who'd been given two helpless cubs in a gift-wrapped box? It was impossible. It was hideous. But I knew that it was true and that Tori was right.

'Clear the set!' Paula shouted helplessly. 'Clear the set!'

Sylvie was in her element, smiling and waving, pressing her face against Gravy's whiskers, tickling Chips under the chin, resting her cheek on the top of Gravy's head and looking wistfully at the photographer's camera. The park was filling up with the public, who started gathering on the fringes of the set, pointing and shouting and taking pictures of their own.

At last, two burly guys with SECURITY printed on their jackets forced their way through the crowd and ushered the journalist and photographer away. Sylvie leaped away from Gravy and started brushing tiger fur off the lapels of her coat.

'She looks like Rabbit did that time she found an old sausage under the kitchen cupboard,' said Tori savagely. 'Really pleased with herself. She set this up. TV stars are like that.'

She said *TV stars* in such a poisonous voice I half expected the grass at our feet to wilt and a toxic green cloud to start billowing around our heads.

'And it's your fault,' Tori suddenly added, whirling round to me.

I took a step backwards, bewildered. 'What?'

'You told that woman about Terry Tanner! You are *such* an idiot, Taya!'

'That's enough, Tori,' said Mum sharply, stepping in between us. 'What's done is done. Apologize to your sister.'

'No,' said Tori, tight-lipped.

I gulped like a tragic fish. 'It's not my fault she's doing this advert, is it? It's a coincidence! OK, so maybe I shouldn't have said anything to her. But Mum told Paula!'

Although Sylvie wasn't fussing over the cubs any more, she was still holding their leads while she talked on her phone. Gravy was looking a bit puzzled, wondering where all the attention had gone.

'And look how confused Gravy is,' Tori said in disgust. 'One minute he's being kissed to death, and the next minute he's invisible. That's tiger abuse. *Extra* tiger abuse, on top of everything else that woman's put them through. Sylvester Spock ought to be asking *her* all those questions about animal welfare, not us.'

Chips started miaowing for Mum. Looking totally unconcerned at the bomb she'd dropped, Sylvie shut her phone and handed the leads back to Dad.

'Take five for hair and make-up, Paula?' she said.

Without waiting for an answer she headed to her trailer, her phone back against her ear. Hair and make-up assistants rushed after her.

'You still haven't apologized to your sister, Tori,' said Dad, recovering his poise.

Tori struggled to get her temper back under control. It was the strangest thing, seeing my sister losing it. She was always really controlled about everything. 'Sorry, Taya,' she said at last. 'But it was a really stupid thing to do, shooting your mouth off like that.'

'I know,' I said in a small voice.

I wish I wasn't always such a div.

With nothing else to do, we took the cubs back to the van for a drink and a cuddle. I dreaded Sylvie coming over and demanding the cubs back on the spot, but she didn't. Which was weird, seeing how passionate she'd been for the journalist.

It was nearly five to twelve by the time Sylvie finally re-emerged from her trailer, make-up and hair perfect once again. Paula looked like she wanted to chew her way through the electric cables snaking everywhere.

'No time left,' she said in a strangled voice. 'It's a *wrap* for today. Same time *tomorrow*, everyone. We have a *lot* left to do.'

The film and lighting guys started unhooking cables, wires and plugs, dismantling the camera tracks and loading their stuff into the three big lorries they'd brought with them, ready to do it all again in the morning.

'*Sorry* about this,' Paula said, coming over to us. 'I had *hoped* to get the tiger shots done *today*, but now . . .' She looked in need of a massage and a sticky toffee pudding. 'Who'd have *thought* she was the lady you were *telling* me about, Anita! I *do* hope she's not going to cause *too* much trouble for you. Listen, can you stay *overnight*? Then we can start *bang* on time in the morning. Stay where you like but make sure it's as *close* as possible so we have *no* delays in the morning. Send the bill to me.' She shot an unprintable look at Sylvie Dickens, who was getting into a zippy little convertible car and laughing on her phone.

All the horrible stuff of the day disappeared up the hoover of forgetfulness. OK, not entirely. But enough.

'A night in London!' I gasped. 'That is *so* cool! Can we stay, Dad?'

Dad scratched his beard, which meant he was tempted. Mum was too, from the gleam in her eyes.

'What about the cubs?' Dad said at last.

We all gazed at the cloud of exhaust spewing from Sylvie Dickens's little car as she sped out of the park.

'She doesn't seem very worried about giving her little treasures somewhere to sleep tonight,' said Mum sourly.

'Any decent hotel would take two titchy tiger cubs,' Tori said. 'It's not like they're much trouble, as long as they can use the bath and the hotel has plenty of extra duvets in case ours get chewed.'

Ignoring this perfectly sensible suggestion, Mum phoned her friend Tamij at London Zoo and arranged for Chips and Gravy to go there. Then she called Joe's dad to ask if they could keep Rabbit for the night and check on the snakes in the morning.

'So,' said Dad, when Mum had arranged everything. 'Now all that remains is to sort out where to stay. The nearest hotel must be the Bilborough.'

Tori frowned. 'Isn't that really expensive?'

'The film production company is paying,' Dad pointed out. 'And it is the closest. So the Bilborough it is.'

I felt like I was in a dream. Stars stayed at the Bilborough, and rich oil billionaires and ladies with small dogs tucked into designer handbags . . . and, apparently, us.

It was a shame that Sylvie Dickens had ruined what should have been a perfect day.

We settled the cubs at London Zoo first with Mum's friend Tamij. She'd fostered animals for Tamij back when he'd worked at Wild World, including a tiny squirrel monkey that had been so naughty Tor and I had named him Naughty. (To be fair, we'd only been six at the time.) Then we went to the Bilborough, parking the van in the basement and taking the lift to reception.

Reception was full of the quiet humming of a very busy and expensive place. All the women were wearing more gold than Tutankhamun and a large guy in a fantastic red and white headdress and long white gown was striding out of the doors and climbing into a slim white limo parked outside. I was pleased to see Mum taking off her hat.

'I am sorry, sir,' said the guy on the reception desk, 'but we can only give you a suite.'

For a minute, I thought he meant a *sweet*. Like a Snickers or a bag of Haribo. I even looked at the bowl of posh-looking mints by the bell that Tori had rung in an important way to get the receptionist's attention.

'A suite will be fine,' said Dad in a high voice.

'Can someone take your bags?' the receptionist enquired. He was well smooth, with a grey waistcoat, black tailcoat and a deep purple tie.

'No bags,' said Mum.

Mum seemed a lot more comfortable in the Bilborough than someone with mud on their boots ought to be. As she tipped the lad who took us up in a rocket-like lift and unlocked our door for us, I wondered about her jetsetting former life as a model. It was hard to get my head around the idea that Mum had had such a different life before we were born.

Walking into the suite felt like walking on to a stage. Everything was totally glam, in creams and greens and yellows. There was a row of windows all along one wall of the main living area, two bedrooms off to the side and a bathroom too. Tori went straight out on to the balcony to goggle at the view. I followed more cautiously. Heights aren't really my thing.

Our balcony joined on to two other balconies, one on either side. Our neighbours were probably footballers, or models, or prime ministers. How crazy was that?

'This is unbelievable!' Tori said. 'You can even see the Science Museum!'

I was still feeling bad about everything that had happened with Sylvie Dickens and how Tori had spoken to me in the park. 'Trust you to look for the Science Museum,' I muttered.

Tori did this strange lunge that ended up with her arms tangled round me. I think it was supposed to be a hug.

'Whoa!' I spluttered, almost losing my balance. 'What are you trying to do, throw me off the balcony? That would be a good way to get rid of your idiotic sister, wouldn't it?'

'I'm sorry I got so mad,' Tori said, letting go. 'But

seeing that woman drooling over the cubs . . . I just lost it.'

'I noticed,' I said. 'It was weird. You never lose it.'

'Never say never.' Tori gave me a cautious smile. 'Mates again?'

'I'll think about it,' I said, as graciously as I could.

Then, doing my best not to look down, I trained my eyes on the horizon in case I could see London Zoo and maybe a pair of titchy stripy tails.

Mum was putting down the phone when we came back into the suite. In the background, Dad had flopped on the sofa and started channel-surfing on the huge telly in the corner.

'Who was on the phone, Mum?' I asked.

'That was my old friend the hotel manager,' said Mum with an airy wave of one hand, like she had loads of friends who were managers of posh hotels. 'He has offered us complimentary use of the spa this afternoon. They don't usually allow children, but he has booked us a special room. Do you want to come? It might cheer us up a little.'

'The Bilborough used your mother for a modelling campaign in the mid-nineties,' Dad explained, grinning at our amazement. 'Looks like they remember her.'

# 19

## Is It True?

Massaged and scrubbed, bathed and primped, polished and buffed, I was feeling a whole lot better now that I was the proud owner of a set of perfect pearly pink fingernails. Mum and I even persuaded Tori to have her nails done, which she agreed to only when she saw they had silver polish that made the tips of her fingers look like they belonged to a robot.

We mooched around Oxford Street after the spa, had tea back at the hotel and ate from room service. We were all so tired from the dramas of the day that we hit our beds and slept like exhausted logs all night long. Well, till five o'clock anyway. Yawning and stumbling around at our alarm call, we climbed out of our huge feather beds and took turns in the bathroom.

'All that's missing is our animals,' Tori said as a lady wheeled in a breakfast trolley of eggs, bacon, fresh orange juice, coffee and croissants, and a healthier breakfast for Dad, complete with a grilled low-salt kipper and granary toast.

'Chips would have ripped my duvet to shreds,' I said. 'Gravy would have hogged all the bathwater. Rabbit would have done some terrible bumskids on this dead expensive carpet and Fernando and Sufi would have scared the breakfast lady senseless. Yeah, well relaxing.'

We both giggled. It was good, being mates again.

'We have to leave in fifteen minutes,' Mum said. 'Eat quickly. Tamij and the cubs are waiting.'

After her spa pampering, Mum looked mind-bogglingly fabulous, even in her purple Bilborough dressing gown. But then she went and reached for her old brown trousers and put them on before shoving her lovely hair back into her hat.

'Mum's hardly going to glam up for another day in Hyde Park,' Tori reminded me, having caught my despairing glance. 'It's not like the cubs care what she looks like.'

Dad gave himself a quick injection of insulin, clicked a couple of sweeteners into his coffee and forked up a mouthful of kipper as he picked up the paper that had come with the breakfast trolley. Then he choked on his coffee and started waving the paper at us. Tori grabbed it out of Dad's hands and stared at the huge photograph plastered across the page.

'Omigosh, it's the CUBS!' she gasped.

TIGERS ARE MY WORLD, said the headline.

'World-renowned model and reality-show presenter Sylvie Dickens (29) shared exclusively with the *News on Sunday* her tearful reunion with two young tiger cubs she had fostered as newborns.'

'Fostered!' Mum snarled. 'Almost *murdered*.'

I snatched the paper off Tori and dashed to the far side of the suite, nimbly dodging my twin as I gawped at the pictures of the cublings being cuddled by Sylvie.

'Our tigers are famous!' I yelled.

'Give it!' Tori demanded. 'I want to see what that woman has to say!'

'Won't,' I said, grinning and waving the paper in the air. Although I'd more or less forgiven my sister for being horrible to me yesterday, a little revenge wouldn't do her any harm.

'Clothes on!' Mum snatched the paper and folded it up firmly, tucking it into her bulky jacket pocket.

'We cannot be late today.'

It was easy getting dressed when you had to put on the same things you wore yesterday. Mum had washed everyone's pants last night and hung them to dry. It was probably the first time the Bilborough radiators had seen Fernleigh Market knickers. We rode down in the lift together, with me trying to sneak a peek at the paper in Mum's pocket and clutching myself with glee every couple of floors.

Out in reception everything was quiet, except for a dark-haired man in a hideous pale-grey suit checking out at the reception desk. As he turned his head to pull something from his pocket, Mum stiffened. She flung out her arm and dragged us all into a dark corner of the reception, out of the grey-suited man's eyeline.

'What?.' said Dad.

'By the desk,' Mum hissed. 'Nobody move until he leaves.'

'What's going on?' Tori said as Dad stiffened as well.

'It's *that man*,' said Mum.

We'd never seen Terry Tanner before. In my imagination, he had a snouty nose and pink trotters for hands, evil little eyes and no hair at all. The reality was a shock. He had a smooth face like a polished dining-room table, large brown eyes and a whole load of jet-black hair gelled back in this thick, shiny wave. I peered out in fascinated horror as he put his wallet back in his pocket and turned for the hotel doors.

'Tez!'

We pulled back even further as Sylvie Dickens came hurrying through the revolving doors into the reception.

Terry Tanner looked shocked by the sudden appearance of his wife. He glanced around furtively and lowered his voice. 'What are you doing here, Sylvie?'

Sylvie fluttered her eyelashes at him. 'I haven't seen you for weeks, babe! Your secretary told me you'd be here this morning. Don't be cross with her for being unable to resist the Sylvie Dickens charm.'

Terry Tanner proceeded to give Sylvie the biggest smooch I've ever seen.

'You seen the papers, Tez?' said Sylvie, pulling back and whipping out her lippy to repair the damage. 'My phone's been ringing off the hook and it's not even six o'clock. You wouldn't have believed it, seeing our babies on the set like some magic publicity fairy had put them there. And you know the family that safari park keeps banging on about being the best carers they've ever used? The ones who are keeping the cubs? They were there! The dad looked like a gorilla, while the mum was a joke in dungarees. And the kids! Ugly little blighters. I felt a bit sorry for them, to be honest.'

Somehow Dad kept a hold of Mum when Sylvie said about the dungarees. If he'd let go, there'd have been a catfight right there on the gold and purple reception rug. And then Tori had to hold on to me when she described us as ugly.

'Great news, doll.' Terry was extracting himself from Sylvie's octopus arms now. 'Listen, I gotta go. I'm not supposed to be here—'

Sylvie pouted. 'Haven't you got time for a cup of tea with your wifey? I've got even better news for you.'

She leaned in and whispered something that made him smile. They headed for the revolving doors arm in arm, where Terry Tanner tipped the doorman. Then they both got into a black car that was waiting outside, and drove away.

We all concentrated on breathing for a couple of minutes.

'I bet they're going to get the cubs,' Tori said.

I gasped. So did Dad.

'They don't know where they are,' Mum said uncertainly.

'Of course they do, Mum!' I said in anguish.

'Sylvie would've found out! That's what she just whispered to him!'

'Tamij won't let that man near the cubs,' said Mum in a voice of pure steel.

I suddenly had a desperate urge to get to London Zoo, to make sure Chips and Gravy were safe. As Dad sorted out the bill, I was already pressing the lift button that would take us down to the car park. We reached the van at a run. Dad started the engine. The noise was dead loud in the morning silence.

Dad drove as fast as he dared through the silent Sunday streets. At the chilly dawn gates to London Zoo, a group of photographers huddled together like seals on an ice floe. I wondered absently what they were waiting for, before hunting the pavements for Sylvie Dickens, Terry Tanner and a big black car. I saw nothing. I could hardly speak with relief.

Gravy almost did a somersault of delight when he saw us coming, *vuvuv*ing madly. Chips actually ran up the side of his cage and did a kind of sideways flip to get down again, landing on Gravy's tail and earning himself a growl.

'So the cubs are famous, hey?' said Tamij, unlocking the cage and letting us in. 'I saw the headline in the paper. Did you see the photographers at the gate?'

'They were for *us*?' I gasped.

'Tamij, has a Mr Tanner been in touch about the cubs?' Dad asked.

Tamij shook his head.

'Thank you,' Mum said with relief. 'Now our morning can really begin.'

The cubs didn't need much grooming today. The straw they'd slept on was clean, and we only had to brush them down and give them a bit of breakfast before we were heading back to the van. We had half an hour to get to Hyde Park.

As we pulled out of the gates, a tide of photographers engulfed us. Flashbulbs exploded in our faces. Dad flung his arm up to shield his eyes from the brightness and almost drove into the gateposts as the van was brought to a standstill. In the back, Chips and Gravy sat up with interest.

'Tell us about the cubs, Mrs Wild!'

'This way, Mr Wild! Kids, look over here!'

Tori looked frightened, Mum looked fed up and Dad simply looked stunned. What was the matter with them all? This was our big moment!

'I'm winding the window down,' I announced. No way was I going to miss my big chance of stardom.

'What's your name, love?' asked a journalist,

thrusting his microphone in my face.

'Taya Sonia Soares Wild,' I announced, pronouncing the Soares bit carefully because everyone always spelt it wrong. I imagined my name in bold on the front page, me cuddling the cubs and telling the world the truth about Sylvie Dickens. I would—

'Is it true that you keep your animals in cramped cages?' the journalist demanded, sticking his microphone so close now that he was practically ramming it up my nostril. 'Is it true that Animal Welfare have been trying to shut you down for years? Is it? Is it true?'

# 20

## Herding Cats

It took us ages to shake off the scorpions and poisonous spiders pretending to be serious journalists, and we were now late for filming. Their awful questions kept jogging through my head like two boxers chasing each other around a boxing ring. Do you mistreat your animals – *biff!* Do you think it's fair to make animals perform for money – *pow!* When will you return the cubs to their rightful owners, Sylvie Dickens and Terry Tanner – *clunk!* Never, I thought fiercely. Nevernevernever. They could knock us out and stamp on our heads and ring their little bell all they liked, but we wouldn't give the Tanners a thing.

Taya was the first one to speak as we turned in to Park Lane.

'I think Dad ran over a photographer's foot.'

'Good,' I said bitterly. 'I hope he smashed his camera too.'

Mum had her nose in the paper and was trying to read it by the streetlights filtering through the van windows.

'That woman is talking here about how losing the cubs was all a terrible misunderstanding, and that she spends her life working for tiger charities!' she said in astonishment.

'Anonymously, of course,' Dad said grimly. 'So no one can check.'

Mum dropped the paper like it was on fire. 'How can a paper print these lies?' she demanded.

'This story must have been Sylvie's "better news",' I said. 'What she whispered to Terry Tanner at the hotel. Making us look like we're cruel to the cubs so they can take them back more easily.'

'It's all for publicity,' said Tori. 'You heard her at the hotel. She doesn't care about the cubs. She only cares about her image.' She glared at me as Mum pulled out her phone and called Wild World for an update. 'You shouldn't have wound down the window and spoken to the journalists, Taya.'

'So it's my fault again, is it?' I demanded, my chin

wobbling. 'How was I supposed to know they'd say such horrible things?'

'It *is* your fault,' Tori said. 'As usual.'

'Be quiet, Tori,' snapped Mum, covering the receiver with her hand.

Yesterday's nightmare and now this? Everything suddenly got on top of me. Dad's illness; the awful terror of losing Chips and Gravy; how we almost had to move house; our scary school and all the changes we'd been through . . . I burst into tears.

'I'm sorry!' I sobbed. 'I can't believe I thought Sylvie Dickens was nice! She's . . . she's . . .' I struggled to think of something bad enough to describe my new least favourite person on the planet. I couldn't think of a single adjective that even began to cover it. There was a flash of more cameras as we entered the park. Journalists were here too.

'I don't want to get out of the car,' said Tori. 'I want to take the cubs home.'

Dad parked the van, leaned over the back and took our hands in his two hairy mitts. 'We have to face them,' he said. 'These terrible claims about us mistreating our animals won't go away unless we do.'

We left the cubs safely in the darkness of the van and walked down to the water's edge to find Paula. Every now and then a photographer surged up to us and took a picture, before getting swatted away by a security guy. We kept our eyes down and did our best not to listen to the horrible questions they were firing at us.

'I'm *so* sorry,' Paula the director said helplessly as we finally reached the edge of the Serpentine. 'Such *dreadful* stories. I don't believe a *word* of it, of course. *Anyone* can see how well cared for the cubs are.'

'Thank you, Paula,' said Mum gratefully.

'I'm sorry we're late for filming,' said Dad.

Paula sighed. 'You're not the *only* ones,' she said. 'There's absolutely *no* sign of Sylvie.'

A few moments later there was an explosion of cameras as Sylvie Dickens drew up in her neat pink convertible with a squeal of tyres. Terry Tanner wasn't with her. She waved and posed before getting out of the car and walking over to her trailer for hair and make-up.

'Funny how someone so passionate about tigers has a fur collar on her coat today,' Tori said coldly.

'Can't you sack her, Paula?' I pleaded. 'It must be illegal, what she's doing.'

'I *wish* I could,' Paula sighed. 'But she's got a contract that says I *can't*.' She turned to the security guys hovering over us like enormous helicopters in yellow jackets. 'Do what you can to keep the press *away*,' she begged them. 'We *have* to finish shooting this ad *today*.'

Trying to keep the photographers away was a full-time job. At least we weren't giving them any shots of the cubs, who were still safely tucked up in the van. So they were focusing their attention on Sylvie instead, despite Security's best efforts to get rid of them.

'It's like herding cats,' Tori said as we watched a photographer creep around a bush and position himself by the water for the third time, his lens trained on Sylvie's trailer. 'Hopeless.'

At last, as the sun rose over the horizon and flooded the park with deep yellow light, Sylvie's trailer door opened. The *Catwalk Talk* star – or Death Star, as Tori had started calling her – appeared in her lovely red coat, smiling and blowing kisses at the photographers, who went mental all over again.

'Can we *please* try some tiger shots?' called Paula in despair over the chaos.

I didn't want that woman anywhere near the cublings. But for Paula's sake, Tori and I helped Mum get the cubs out of their cage. There was a blast of photographs somewhere behind us, and a few choice swear words as a security guy hustled a photographer away from our van. We brushed the cubs' coats, gave them a drink of water and brought them down to the water's edge on their special leads, where Kalim checked them over just as he had the day before. Then Dad attempted to explain the leads to Sylvie one more time as she preened at the cameras, a peacock in a red wool coat.

Looking like he was sucking a lemon, Sylvester Spock and his clipboard advanced towards us and Mum.

'Not very good coverage for you this morning, Mrs Wild,' he said.

Mum fixed him with her flat-eye look, the one like a cat on the point of savaging your wrist as you're stroking it.

'Animals UK has taken a dim view of this story,' Sylvester Spock continued, oblivious to the danger he was in. 'Animals cannot exhibit their natural behaviour in cages that are too small. Cages that are too small contravene every rule in the book.'

Mum whispered something in Portuguese that sounded like a dreadful hissing curse, but which was in fact the first two lines from a rhyme she used to sing to me and Tori when we were little. Now I came to think of it, it was about a stork.

Sylvester Spock adjusted his collar and looked uncomfortable. 'Mrs Wild, I am merely telling you—'

'*Thank* you, Mr Spock!' Paula called loudly. 'We'll discuss your concerns *later*. Now we need the cubs for filming. Kalim *has* signed them off as fit for work, and as agreed yesterday, the *paperwork* is all in order. *Positions*, please! Sylvie? Sylvie!'

Reluctantly, Sylvie Dickens turned away from the cameras. Once again the security guards tried to usher the journalists away. One of the guards caught a journalist by the scruff of his leather jacket and dragged him off like one of those wheelie bags old ladies use in supermarkets, his heels squealing on the tarmac.

'Shirley Dickens is starting to get on my nerves,' said Tori, chewing the end of her plait.

'Only starting?' I said in a hollow voice, unable to find the energy to correct Tori on Sylvie's name.

'ACTION!' Paula shouted.

Sylvie minced up to the edge of the lake, holding the cubs' leads between two fingers. The camera ran beside her on its little traintracks. The cubs flowed after her like stripy smoke, their eyes trained on Mum and the bucket of meat just out of shot.

'*Great!*' Paula called. 'Going *well*, Sylvie! Keep it up!'

'Good boy, Chips!' Mum called. 'Come on, Gravy! Nearly beef time!'

Chips suddenly clocked the lake in all its lovely wide wetness. Beside his brother, Gravy's whiskers twitched.

Tori took her plait out of her mouth. 'You know what I'm wishing?'

I knew, like I often do with Tori, exactly what it was that she was wishing. Because I was wishing it too. I was wishing it so hard I half expected sparks to shoot out of my ears.

'And . . . release,' said Paula.

Sylvie pressed haphazardly at the leads. Nothing happened. Chips stopped dead, sniffing the water hard. Gravy bumped into him. Sylvie tugged. Nothing.

*Go on, cublings*, I thought. *You know you want to*.

'Release?' said Paula again. 'Release, Sylvie . . . *RELEASE!*'

The cubs sprang gracefully into the lake. Their leads went taut. Screeching and swearing and stabbing madly at the buttons on the leads, Sylvie Dickens cartwheeled in head first after them. Her coat and skirt flipped down over her glossy copper head and flashed her pants at the world for half a second before the great and glorious splosh that drenched half the camera crew and made my life totally worth living all over again.

'Nice knickers,' said Tori. 'I wonder why she didn't just let go?'

The photographers from earlier started popping up like ducks in a shooting gallery from behind every bush and car in sight.

'No cameras!' Sylvie screamed. Her hair hung tragically over to one side in a dead unflattering style as she flapped about in the water. 'I'll sue anyone who publishes this!'

Chips and Gravy were swimming right out into the lake. Chips reached the island in the middle, pulled his long wet body out of the water and shook himself. Gravy scrambled out after him. The cubs both started licking each other as if to say 'Excellent swim' and then flopped down with their long tongues hanging out and their leads trailing on the ground beside them. I was laughing so hard, I was folded up like a deckchair. It was totally and completely the BEST thing I'd ever seen.

Tori however saw things from a slightly more important angle.

'OK,' she said, frowning as she stared at Chips and Gravy on the island across the wide water of the Serpentine. 'So how do we get the cubs back again?'

# 21

## My Lawyers Will Grate You Like Cheese

The fabulous, wonderful giggles that had practically been ripping me in half dried up very suddenly. As usual, Tori had a point. The cubs were still very little. It had been a long swim to the island for them both. There was no way they could make it all the way back again by themselves. It was like asking an elephant to do a plié, or me to recite my eight-times table without going wrong.

Chips cocked his head to one side, as if trying to work out how to reach us for beef and cuddles.

'No!' I shouted, starting forward in horror as he splashed clumsily back into the lake with his eyes trained on us. Gravy got up from the sandy shore as

177

well and followed his brother into the water.

'Get OFF me, you oafs!' Sylvie was screeching as she flailed about in the lake, whacking away any hands that were reaching out to help her. 'My hair! My *shoes*!'

We didn't give a stuff for Sylvie Dickens and her shoes. We had more important things to worry about.

'They'll never make it,' Tori moaned, holding her hands to her mouth. 'What are we going to do?'

The cubs were nearly a third of the way across now, but they were both tiring and starting to swim in confused circles. People were gathering on the shores of the lake, snapping photos with their phones.

'I'm coming, Chips! Hang on, Gravy!' Tori kicked off her trainers as if she was about to leap in like one of those people who swim the Serpentine on Christmas Day. 'Are you coming?' she demanded over her shoulder at me. Her eyes were mad.

'Don't be daft, Tori!' I gasped, feeling more than a little freaked. My sensible sister *never* did reckless stuff like leaping into lakes with her clothes on. 'You've only got your fifty-metre badge and I can't swim at all!'

'They're going to drown unless we help them!' Tori cried.

Chips, followed of course by Gravy, made the sensible decision to swim back to the island, which was a lot closer than the main shore. The cubs paddled slowly through the water until they reached dry land, both looking seriously knackered now. The concrete slab of panic lifted off my shoulders, leaving me dizzy with relief.

'OK,' said Tori, calming down a little. She put her trainers back on and straightened her plait. '*Now* we can think. Where's Dad?'

I pointed to the water's edge. In the middle of the crowd of confused film crew members and overexcited journalists and wet actresses, Dad was arguing with a plum-coloured Sylvester Spock. He hadn't seen the problem.

'What about Mum?' said Tori.

'No idea,' I said, starting to feel desperate. 'I think she went to find some towels when she saw the cubs dive in.'

Tori chewed urgently on her plait again. 'They're going to try and swim again in a minute,' she said.

My eye fell on the pedalos moored by the lake café. 'How about those?' I said, and pointed. 'We can pedal out and fetch them.'

Tori boggled at me. 'A pedalo?'

I wasn't sure if my sister looked impressed or depressed. Or whatever the opposite of impressed is.

'Not one pedalo,' I said, keen to show Tori that I had at least half a brain. 'Two. We pedal out, pick up a cub each and pedal back again.'

'Taya,' said my sister after a very long pause, 'that's such a mad idea, it's a stroke of genius.'

I looked cautiously at her. 'Seriously? You think it's a good idea?'

'It's a *fantastic* idea,' said Tori with this blazing look in her eyes.

I inflated like one of those frogs you see on David Attenborough. My brainy twin sister thought I'd had a good idea! This was my chance to make up for all the stupid things I'd managed to do in the last two days.

The sound of the cubs miaowing for help floated across the lake.

'We have to do this ourselves,' said Tori, making a decision. 'There's no time to tell Mum or Dad.'

She started running around the edge of the lake. A bit like the way Gravy always copied Chips, I followed. By the time we reached the pedalo hire place, Chips was back in the water, keeping close to the edge of the island while chasing a duck and splashing about with his massive paws. The duck was going mental, flapping its wings and quacking its beak off. I suppose ducks don't get chased by tigers very often.

'At least Chips is enjoying himself now,' I said.

'The duck isn't,' Tori pointed out.

It was too early for the pedalo hire place to be open. Tori marched down the jetty and helped herself, with me hopping and running beside her.

The duck had made it past Chips and on to the island. It practically fainted when it saw Gravy on the shore and threw itself back into the lake like a feathery bomb. You had to feel sorry for it, even though it was hilarious.

We climbed into our pedalos and set off. The wash from Tori's pedalo kept sloshing over my feet. I tried very hard not to think about all the people watching us or the deep green water churning away underneath me. I hadn't learned to swim yet. To take my mind off drowning, I fixed my eyes on the cubs. I was so crazy about them, it actually hurt. Having a surname like Wild maybe means you're destined to love animals with all your heart. I don't know. But it felt that way to me.

We reached them after ten minutes. My legs were aching like mad. The cubs *vuvuv*ed with delight when they saw us. Tori reached down and grabbed Chips by the scruff of his sopping-wet neck, hauling him up into the pedalo beside her. He butted against her so hard she almost lost her balance and tipped off the back. 'Taya, get Gravy!' she shouted at me.

I took a deep breath, braced myself against the pedalo and leaned over the water as far as I dared, stretching out my fingers towards Gravy.

*Please may I not fall in and drown and die and embarrass myself,* I prayed.

Gravy made life a whole lot easier by jumping into the pedalo by himself, soaking my clothes in a flash and turning me into a shivering wreck on account of the cold as well as the basic terror. The pedalo rocked like mad, making me feel more than a bit queasy.

'Sit,' I ordered hysterically.

Gravy did as he was told, resting his head on my lap. I thanked all the gods and angels and fairies in the world that I didn't have the far naughtier Chips.

And so we started pedalling back. Two sisters, two tiger cubs, two pairs of extremely wet pants and probably a million goosebumps between us. About halfway across, Chips decided to stand on the front of Tori's pedalo like the angel on the front of a Rolls-Royce. Gravy stayed pressed up against me so closely that I could feel the warmth of his skin through his wet fur. It was the only thing that kept me going.

I was so exhausted when we reached the main shore

that my legs kept pedalling by themselves, even though all I was doing was bumping against the jetty.

'We made it,' I heard Tori say. 'You can stop pedalling now, Taya.'

Cameras blasted off on all sides, but now they were aimed at us instead of Sylvie Dickens. Dad was there, helping me out. Towels had appeared from somewhere, rubbing me down and warming me up. Gravy didn't leave my side for a minute, despite Kalim's best attempts to make sure he was unhurt after his watery adventure. Paula fussed around us both, saying things like 'Unbe*liev*able! Unbe*liev*able!' over and again.

'Tori! Taya! Over here! Give us a smile!'

There were at least ten journalists standing in front of me and my sister and the cubs, holding out microphones. The last time I'd seen them outside London Zoo, they'd looked as mean as a swarm of wasps. Now they were all smiles and jokes. It was a lot to take in.

Mum suddenly came crashing through everyone. Her hat had fallen off, tumbling her chocolate hair everywhere. 'You are heroes!' she gasped. 'My daughters, the heroes!' she shouted triumphantly at the photographers, who went bananas all over again as she attempted to gather me and Tor and both cubs in her frankly way-too-short arms.

'Aren't you Anita Soares?' one of the journalists asked. 'The model?'

Impossibly, the excitement went up another peg. Even more photographs exploded around us. Until . . .

'When you've *quite* finished?'

Sylvie Dickens's voice was small but deadly. Everyone stopped looking at us and looked at her instead. She was wearing a fresh new outfit though her hair was still wet. She looked like she was about to combust on the spot as her eyes sizzled right into poor Paula and her clapperboard.

'I quit,' she hissed. 'And as for *you*,' she added, turning the full force of her fury on Mum and Dad, 'my lawyers will grate you like cheese. And when they're done, you'll be lucky ever to work again!'

# 22

# The Best Sister in the World

'The cubs are cold and Wild and Woolly is ruined and I can't ever watch *Catwalk Talk* again!' I sobbed as once again Sylvie Dickens commanded the attention of the photographers.

'Whatever is Wild and Woolly?' said Dad, rubbing Gravy with the towel while Kalim examined Chips.

'Our business,' I howled. 'I thought of the name when we were on the pedalo because our name is Wild. And my feet are soaking.'

'You're not making sense, Taya,' Mum said gently.

'Tori says I never make sense,' I hiccuped. 'You should be used to it by now. I'm useless and totally freezing cold and I've spoiled everything. Are Sylvie Dickens's lawyers really going to sue you? If Sylvie quits then the whole ad is ruined and you won't get paid for using the cubs and everything will go back to how it was before we had the idea of filming our animals!'

'Don't worry about that,' Dad soothed. Gravy wriggled away from Dad's towel and butted against me, jealously pushing Chips out of the way.

'You may have told Sylvie Dickens a bit too much, but you had the pedalo idea,' Tori said, putting her arm around me. 'You had the animal modelling idea too. You're not useless, Taya. You're brilliant and funny and you just saved our cubs from drowning. You're the best sister in the world.'

I stared at Tori through the film of tears that wobbled across my eyeballs and made me see three of her. 'I'm also going mad because it sounded like you just said something completely lovely and didn't take the mickey out of me once,' I said suspiciously.

'OK,' Tori said. 'How about this? Wild and Woolly is maybe the worst name you've thought of so far. It even beats Oscars and Whiskers.'

I gave a wobbly smile. 'That's better, you cyberdork.' I lunged over to kiss my twin.

'Get away from me,' Tori said, grinning as Gravy started slobbering all over my legs.

There's nothing like annoying your twin and getting

tiger dribble on your clothes to cheer a person up, not to mention the bag of chocolate bars that Mum produced from somewhere. We cuddled the cublings and munched on mini Mars bars and watched the rest of the drama unfolding in front of us. There was nothing else we could do.

The photographers were starting to drift away now, having got enough pictures to wallpaper the M25. Poor Paula was doing her best to ignore the journalists' inquisitive eyes and digital recorders as she tried to make Sylvie stay and complete the Double-Take shoot.

'You'll be associated with *such* a strong product, Sylvie. I'm *sure* we can use a body double to walk the tigers if you're *unhappy* about trying it again. We simply *must* get this in the can by the end of today. Is there *anything* else we can do to make you change your *mind*?'

It happened so quickly I almost missed it. Chips broke away from Mum and trotted over to give Sylvie a sniff. Just a friendly sniff, you understand. She must have smelled quite interesting after her dip in the Serpentine. He was probably trying to say sorry. Caught off guard, Sylvie lashed out at him with her foot, catching him on the nose and making him squeal. A camera flashed.

There was a moment of total silence, like the bit just after Dermot says 'and the winner of this year's *X Factor* is . . .'

'*Miss Dickens*,' cawed Sylvester Spock, flapping and pecking his way through the stunned crowd. 'Animals UK will not stand for—'

'Miss Dickens! Miss—'

'She just kicked it. She kicked that defenceless cub! Sylvie, what have you got to say?'

'I . . .' Sylvie stuttered, losing her perfect poise. 'It . . . Pins and needles . . .'

We rushed over to poor Chips, who was looking dazed and shaking his head. Gravy sniffed anxiously at his brother while Kalim checked Chips for damage.

'Pins and needles!' Tori spluttered as she stroked Chips's head. 'Like anyone's going to believe that!'

'Sylvie!' The journalists suddenly sounded like hungry wolves. 'Do you think your career will survive this mistake? You've lost all credibility with the animal rights lobby. Do you think you'll get the cubs back after this? Will your work with tigers continue? Did it ever, in fact, begin?'

Sylvie Dickens stormed off, the journalists and photographers snapping at her heels. You didn't need to be a genius to work out that her career was in tatters. It was hard to feel sorry for her. Around us, the Double-Take camera crew sighed and muttered and stared at their watches.

'*Now* what am I going to do?' said Paula, almost in tears. 'There's *crew* to pay and only *two hours* left on our licence and absolutely *nothing* to show for it!'

'She is a witch,' Mum spat, glaring after Sylvie's departing back and rubbing Chips's furry nose. 'Good riddance.'

Paula took in Mum in all her angry magnificence. With her hideous hat long forgotten, her chocolate hair blowing in the wind and anger flooding her gorgeous face with fire, Mum looked like a destroying angel.

'Did I hear someone say you used to *model*, Anita?' Paula said.

'She was famous,' I said, lifting my head from where I was nuzzling Chips' ears.

'She modelled for the Bilborough,' Dad put in.

'And she was the face of 1985,' piped up Tori.

Paula clutched at Mum's baggy coat sleeve. 'Is there *any* chance *you* can do this shoot instead of Sylvie, Anita? We'd pay you *extra* for *such* short notice. Could you? Provided the *tigers* are all right, of course . . .'

She looked at Kalim, who smiled at us all reassuringly. 'Chips is fine,' he said. 'Gravy too.'

'In that case, of course I will, Paula,' said Mum in a deep and dignified voice. 'I will show you how it is done. You will never need to use amateurs again.'

Sylvester Spock loomed into view like one of those recurring dreams you have when you get so tangled in your duvet you think you're being eaten by a marshmallow.

'I'm shutting you down!' he shouted, waving his clipboard. 'Cubs being kicked! Cubs loose and unsupervised in the Serpentine! I've seen quite enough!'

After Sylvester Spock had bawled out Sylvie Dickens about Chips, I'd started warming to him. Not any more.

'I thought you were on our side now?' I said, rounding on him. 'It's not our fault Sylvie Dickens kicked him! You should take it up with her, not us!'

'Those animals nearly drowned!' Sylvester Spock spluttered.

'I think you'll find that swimming is exhibiting natural behaviour for tigers, Mr Spock,' said Tori.

It was a good answer. No – more than that. It was a *great* answer. Sylvester Spock had no choice but to tick his little box marked 'exhibiting natural behaviour' and raise his hands and declare we could go ahead and that he only had the cubs' welfare at heart. Which, to be fair, he did.

'Hair!' Paula called briskly. 'Make-up! When you're ready, Anita? Everyone, *go go go*!'

'Mum looks incredible!' I sighed in ecstasy twenty minutes later as Mum emerged from the trailer Sylvie Dickens had recently vacated.

The wind was teasing Mum's long hair into a shiny chocolate cloud. She was wearing an electric-blue coat that set off her gorgeous golden skin, her face flawlessly made up. The male members of the film crew all stood a little taller and started talking in loud, manly voices as they adjusted their camera lenses. Standing with the cubs, Dad looked as dazed as Chips when Sylvie kicked him on the nose.

'Ready for your close-ups, Anita?' called Paula. 'And . . . action!'

Mum nailed it in one. The camera ran along its little track, filming her madly as she pushed her Double-Take hair back from her face and walked up and down.

'Tigers!' called Paula in excitement after half an hour.

Dad rushed over with the freshly dried and groomed cubs while Tori and I watched. His face was as flushed as a schoolkid's as he handed Mum the leads. Good as gold now they had Mum in charge, the cubs walked meekly behind her as Dad waved the beef at them.

'Release the leads!' Paula called.

The leads worked first time. Even more miraculously, the cublings both sat down obediently while Mum walked off without them, and started washing each other's ears in the cutest way imaginable. Paula had to reshoot that bit as all the extras who were supposed to be gawping at Mum took their eyes off her and gawped at the cublings instead. But somehow, the second time went even more smoothly than the first.

'*Gorgeous!*' Paula shouted at last. '*Terrific! Perfect*! It's a *wrap*, everyone. It's a *wrap!*'

# 23

## Plume of Smoke

'WILD ABOUT ANIMALS! Of course! Why didn't we think of that?' said Tori on Monday morning, sitting back from the kitchen table as she banged the headline on page three of the paper. 'Short, sharp and straight to the point!'

Unwilling as I was to admit defeat on my latest brainwave for our family business – Wildly Famous – Tori was right as usual. The journalists had the perfect name for our new business.

'Twisting words is a newspaper's job,' I said a bit ungraciously. 'Ow, Gravy – stop biting my toes!'

Gravy looked up at me sweetly from under the kitchen table. As I bent down to tickle his ears, I smelt something eggy.

'What a stink, Gravy,' I said with a frown. 'Too much beef yesterday, I think.'

'Wild About Animals!' Tori read from the paper. 'A fledgling animal modelling agency got off to a shaky start this weekend with accusations of animal kidnap and cruelty on a shoot in Hyde Park. But the fur flew in quite a different direction when Shirley Dickens (43) lashed out on set at Crisps, a five-month-old tiger cub. It was paws, claws and applause when model turned animal foster carer Anita Wild (39) stepped into the fray and saved the shoot. Go, Anita, we say!' Tori looked up. 'I *knew* she looked like a Shirley.'

'It really says paws, claws and applause?' I asked in delight, forgetting about the eggy smell.

'Some of their facts are dodgy.' Tori's nose was back in the paper. 'Fancy calling Chips "Crisps"! As if! And are you really thirty-nine, Mum?'

'If it says in the newspaper, it must be true,' Mum said, scrubbing hard at the porridge saucepan.

'I recommend the article on page nine,' said Dad.

I took the paper off my twin and rustled it in an important way. I tangled it up so badly that Mum had to get it off me and set it straight, but I got to page nine in the end.

'TERRY TANNER IN TAX TROUBLE,' I read.

'Ooh! Terry Tanner's been a bad boy! It seems he wasn't supposed to be in London this weekend.'

'He said something about that in the hotel, remember?' said Tori.

'Listen to this,' I said, peering closer at the titchy writing in the paper. 'Terry Tanner was over from Jersey – where he lives so he doesn't have to pay any tax, it says here – for a secret meeting with some extremely dodgy accountants at the *Bilborough*!' I lowered the paper and stared at my family. 'I wonder how they knew he was at the Bilborough on Saturday night?'

Mum scrubbed the porridge pot harder.

'No idea,' said Dad.

*Weird*, I thought in wonder. Journalists obviously had serious super powers. They knew *everything*.

'And it says that he's got all these secret businesses in England he hasn't told the government about, so he owes the government loads of money!' Tori went on, reading the article over my shoulder.

'How much?' I said.

Tori showed me. The figure was so eye-watering that I had to blink a couple of times before I could trust my eyes.

'He won't have any extra money to spend on lawyers to get the cubs back now,' said Mum.

'Anyway,' Tori added, 'the cubs aren't as cute as Sylvie remembered, are they?'

'Certainly not since they ducked her in the Serpentine,' I giggled.

'I think we are safe from those two at last,' said Mum with a smile of satisfaction.

Dad's phone started buzzing in his pocket for about the tenth time that morning. 'Wild About Animals?' he said, winking at us as he headed off to his office with the phone clamped to his ear.

It was well funny, hearing Dad use the new name and seeing him in his ripped jeans and *So Sue Me* T-shirt and old trainers and beardy chin sounding like he was in a suit and tie.

Joe came in through the back door, his rucksack threatening to tip him over backwards. Rabbit thumped her tail in greeting.

'Hi!' he said breathlessly. 'I saw the paper. I had to come over so we can all walk to the bus together. I can't believe I know you!'

'You don't,' said Tori. 'Now we're famous we are completely different people. Who are you?'

Joe looked worried. 'I'm Joe,' he said.

'JOKE!' Tor and I both said, laughing like lunatics.

We spent a few minutes collecting our school stuff.

Then we all waved goodbye to Mum, who was getting ready to take the cubs and Rabbit out for their morning walk on Fernleigh Common, and headed out the door, down the drive and into our road. At the top of the road, as we turned right towards our bus stop, I happened to glance to the left. And I saw something that made my blood go cold.

Sauntering towards us were Dwight Dingle and his mates.

'Hello, MORON!' Dwight Dingle said in delight.

We froze. There was no sign of the bus. There was no sign of anyone, actually – we were earlier than normal. What were Dwight Dingle and his mates doing at this end of town?

'Thought we'd come and see you, Moron,' said Dwight. He hitched his trousers up in a menacing kind of way. 'Teach you a bit about respect. We call you Moron, you respond. That's how it works. I don't like this new attitude of yours, pretending that we don't exist. It's rude.'

'Rude,' agreed the dinosaurs behind Dwight.

Joe looked terrified. I looked beseechingly at Tori. She stood up to people like Cazza. She'd stand up to Dwight Dingle with the same courage she showed every time we walked past him at the school gates and dodged his lashing feet. Wouldn't she?

'RUN!' Tori bellowed.

We turned like hares and fled – past the bus stop, past CostQuik and the letter box, past the lamp post and the dodgy fence that always had flyers on for dog obedience classes.

'MO-RON!' cheered the dinosaurs, giving chase.

'Where are we going?' I screamed at Tori.

'The common!' Tori shouted back.

I grabbed Joe's arm and yanked him down the footpath that led off the main road to the wilderness of Fernleigh Common. The blood was pumping in my ears. I forgot everything about the weekend and Sylvie Dickens, Chips and Gravy and Terry Tanner, manicures and soggy red wool coats and pedalos and newspapers. The only thing I had room for in my brain was fear.

The dinosaurs jogged casually behind us, like they had all the time in the world. 'MO-RON!' they called happily.

'I wish I'd never started that positive action thing,' panted Joe, racing along beside me.

'No time for regrets,' I panted back. 'Just keep running.'

Tori was bounding ahead, her long brown plait flying. She was heading for the copse on the common where we'd once made a den. I speeded up, feeling a little more confident about the situation. We could hide in the den. For years, if we had to. We'd hidden a tin of Spam there once, and Tori had even remembered to hide a tin opener with it. We'd survive.

Calls of 'MO-RON! MO-RON!' were growing louder behind us. And I realized with horror that we weren't going to make it to the copse and the den in time.

We could see our house now, the roof peeping over the edge of the trees. I stumbled in shock as Mum appeared on the path before us with Rabbit and the cubs. She looked so gorgeously normal and safe that I almost leaped into her arms with relief.

'Dwight . . . Dingle . . .' Tori panted as Joe raised a long trembling finger to point behind us.

Mum looked bewildered. 'Who?'

It has to be said that I don't have good ideas very often. And I do have a very big mouth that runs away with itself a lot. And maybe I get a bit fixated on fame and popularity. But every now and again, I come out with stuff to be proud of.

'No time to explain, Mum,' I gasped. 'The cubs' leads – quick!'

Still looking flummoxed, Mum handed the leads

over. I thrust them both in Joe's hands. Then I gave him a push so he faced back down the path towards the oncoming charge.

The ground drummed to the sound of feet. Dwight Dingle and his mates galloped around the corner with a cheer. The cubs started with fright. Chips curled his lip and growled, while Gravy crouched and lashed his tail.

The cheering faltered, dwindled and spluttered to nothing as Dwight and his gang processed that fact that Joe stood before them, holding what appeared to be a pair of extremely angry tigers on two leads. Dwight Dingle boggled like one of those rubber toys you squeeze until their eyes pop out.

Tori went to say something. In another moment of unusual brilliance, I grabbed her arm before she intervened. I knew how important it was that Joe did this by himself.

Joe pulled himself up as tall as he could. The cubs had both recovered from their fright and were now sniffing with interest in the dinosaurs' direction. Dwight let out a girly scream.

'The name,' Joe said, 'is Joe Morton. Don't wear it out. In fact, don't use it. Ever.'

\* \* \*

Then, like one of those special-effects moments you get in big-budget movies, there was suddenly the most enormous, spectacular, theatrical BANG you ever heard. Everyone screamed; Dwight Dingle screamed again. And away to Mum's left, we all saw the roof of our house lift like the lid off a bottle of Coke and a plume of smoke scorch the sky.

I stared stupidly, my brain trying to process what it was seeing. Flames – check. Heat – check. Noise – check. And yet I knew none of it was really happening because stuff like this didn't happen to ordinary people like me. It didn't. It *couldn't*.

Our roof came crashing down among the trees off to our left, shocking us all to our senses. Someone screamed 'RUN!' And a thin voice – maybe mine – floated trembling on the smoky air.

'Did . . . our house just blow up?'

# WILD

## WIN a zoo keeper experience!

If you're wild about animals, and want to have fun like Tori and Taya looking after cute and cuddly animals, then enter this exciting competition.

One lucky winner will become a zoo keeper for the day at London Zoo, helping out with everything from meerkats to giraffes – amazing!

To enter just go to

## www.hodderchildrens.co.uk/wild

or send a postcard with your name and address on to:
Wild Competition, Hachette Children's Books,
338 Euston Road, London, NW1 3BH

Closing date: 31st December 2011
Open to UK residents only

*h*
*Hodder*
*Children's*
*Books*